OFF THE RAILS

OFF THE RAILS

A Collection

of

Weird, Wicked, & Wacky Stories

JEROME W. McFADDEN

BETHLEHEM WRITERS GROUP, LLC

OFF THE RAILS

The contents of this publication are works of fiction. Names, characters, places, businesses, organizations, events, and incidents are either the product of the author's imagination or used fictitiously. Any resemblance to actual persons, living or dead, organizations, events, or locales is entirely coincidental.

Cover image, "Train Wreck at Montparnasse 1895" (photographer unknown) is in the public domain.

Interior images used under license from DepositPhotos. com

Trade paperback ISBN: 978-0-9892650-6-5
ebook ISBN: 978-0-9892650-7-2

Library of Congress Control Number: 2019908923

Printed in the United States of America.

To Danielle,

"... whatever is done by only me is your doing ..."

e. e. cummings

Table of Contents

Police Blotter

A Game of Chance

A SINGLE KNOCK on the door.

A voice inside said, "Come in."

Davis stepped into the suite, quietly closing the door behind him. He stopped to survey the room. Plush. Expensive. Beautiful view of Vegas at night. A small kitchen and dining room on the right. Two separate doors on the left. Probably adjacent bedrooms. A nice place to live. Or die.

The man sitting on the sofa in the living room looked at his watch, smiling at him. "Right on time," he said.

Davis couldn't help glancing at his own watch. Ten p.m. As agreed.

"The money and the gun are on the dining room table," the man said. "Or we can do it here, if it makes you more comfortable. A little less formal, so to speak."

Davis scanned the dining room table. A stack of money and a revolver, the rest of the table clear. He couldn't resist commenting, "The bathroom might be better. Easier to clean up afterward, if there is an afterward."

The man stood up to walk into the dining area. "No need to worry about cleanup. The room has been paid for in cash, under a false name, of course. I would ask you to reimburse me for half the cost of the room, before we start the game. I would also ask you to put on these rubber gloves and use this towel to wipe the doorknob inside and out, and any other portion of the door that you may have touched."

Davis accepted the gloves and the small hand towel offered to him. He had not noticed the man was wearing a set of rubber gloves until now. As he turned to wipe down the door and the knobs, the man said, "I assume you have been discreet coming into the hotel. That no one may have noticed you."

"I took a taxi and walked from a block away. I doubt if anybody noticed me coming through the lobby. It was busy."

The man sat at the table, in the middle, so that they would be face to face. "That's fine. Keep your gloves on."

Davis sat down, glancing at the gun and the stack of money. He couldn't help but stare.

"Do you have your wager?" the man asked. Davis took an envelope from his jacket and placed it on the table, on the other side of the gun. "Do you want to count it?" he asked.

The man smiled. "You wouldn't want to short me."

"How much for my share of the room, or should I say suite?"

"Four hundred and ninety dollars and eighty-nine cents."

Davis pulled out his wallet and counted out five $100 bills. "Keep the change. A touch expensive for an hour's use of the room."

"If we last that long," the man replied as he raked in the $500. "Feel free to take this five hundred back, if I lose," he said. He then opened the envelope to stack Davis' money on the table, next to the gun. He took out a cigarette lighter to burn the envelope, shaking the ashes into a wastebasket as the paper flared in flames. He looked up, asking, "You know the rules?"

"It's not that complicated."

The man frowned, as if displeased with the witticism. "There is fifty thousand in each stack. Winner take all. We continue directly through all six rounds. If you feel it necessary to spin the cylinder again, after we start, you lose. If you chicken out before we begin, you lose. And of course, if you die, you lose."

"And if one of us dies, the other one calls housekeeping for clean up?"

The man dismissed the question with a wave of his hand. "You just walk out. The housekeeper will find the corpse in the morning. There is no connection to either you or me. Take the money and walk. Try not to run, as you might call attention to yourself."

"And the gun?"

The man picked up the gun, holding it by the barrel, the butt towards Davis. "As you can see, the serial number has been filed off. It's a cheap gun. But good enough to hit your temple accurately from two inches. Do with it whatever you want. Take it or leave it. If you win, of course."

Davis said, "You've done this before."

"Or I wouldn't be here."

"And if you lose this time?"

"Game's over, for me. You could take over the game if you want. The word will get out. There are always takers."

Davis nodded, as if understanding the reasoning behind that statement. But he knew he would never do this again. The longer he sat here, the more terrified he was becoming. One game would be enough, if he could hold himself together.

The man continued to hold the gun in the neutral position. He flipped out the cylinder and spun it to show there were no bullets in it. "I will now put one bullet in it. Or you can put the bullet in it, if you prefer. Then we will spin it once again. Or as many times as you like. Then we play."

Davis stared at the gun. "And if I take this gun and shoot you and run away?"

The man smiled again. "You would have one sixth of a chance of having the bullet in the chamber as you fired. Odds of sixteen-point-seven percent. Then it would get ugly. I would beat the shit out of you. If you did manage to be lucky with the first shot, people would come after you, as it would be obvious I did not have the gun against my temple at the time of the shot."

"Who would come after me?"

"The people who set this up for you. I am not a stupid man, you know."

The man was obviously not stupid. He had an intelligent face, good manners, was well dressed—the appearance of being well off and well educated.

"Shall we begin?" the man asked. He handed a bullet across the table. "Would you like to load?"

Davis accepted the bullet, and took the gun, his hands trembling. He fumbled trying to slide the round into the cylinder but finally managed to thread it into the hole. The man acted as if he did not notice the small flounder. Davis appreciated that.

"W-who starts?"

The man reached into his slacks to pull out a coin, tapping it on the edge as he put in on the table. "It's only fair to flip for it, no? To start a game of chance, we should start with another game of chance. Sorry it's only a nickel. We should be using a quarter or maybe a gold casino chip, something a greater value than a measly five cents when we're playing for so much money. Oh well . . ."

"W-who calls it?" Davis asked.

"Oh, I will let you call it. I will even let you flip it, just to see how your luck is going tonight."

Davis knew the man was mocking him, trying to sap his confidence. Part of the game. He would ignore it. "Heads."

The nickel bounced down the table and the man slapped his hand on it, then raised it up. He didn't bother to glance down. Instead he gazed across the table at Davis as if not caring one way or the other. "And?" he said.

"Heads."

"How nice. You get to begin."

Davis picked up the gun. Smith & Wesson, Model 10, .38. An older gun. The plastic handle slightly cracked. One hundred thousand dollars and death on the line and they were using a cheap "Saturday night special." How ironic. He felt stupid asking but couldn't stop himself. "I don't suppose I could test fire it once, just to get the feel of it?"

The man laughed for the first time that evening and looked around. "I don't think the hotel would appreciate us shooting holes in their walls or windows and we wouldn't want a stray shot to hurt an innocent person. You won the toss, you have the gun, you have the advantage, for the moment. But I will be happy to start, if you want to see how it is done."

Davis sat frozen, the gun in his hand. He had asked for this, he had searched it out: the high stakes, the ultimate gamble, a quick solution, one way or another, to his money problems. Just spin the cylinder, put the gun to his head, and pull the trigger. Just . . . do it.

His hand wobbled. The cold metal touched his temple. He pulled it away slightly to resettle it close enough to his head so that he could feel its presence but not touch his skin. He closed his eyes. And pulled the trigger.

Click.

The sense of being alive washed through him in a flood of effervescent warm liquid, filling every inch of his body from the top of his head to the end of his toes. The joy of being alive.

"Well, good for you," the man said, reaching across to take the gun. "You have balls. Now it's my turn. But my odds are still good, you know? One out of five now, eighty percent in my favor. Better than I would get at the tables."

Click.

"Oh, now we're down to seventy-five percent. One out of four. Still strong odds but somewhat chancy," he said, handing the gun back to Davis.

Who almost dropped it.

The gun suddenly took on a life of its own, wobbling and diving up and down and sideways in erratic circles, as if not wanting to go near the side of his head. The man watched but said nothing.

Davis forced it to the side of his head.

Click.

The man reached over to take back the gun. "Ah, it's getting serious now, isn't it?" he said. "Three shots left. One out of three. Sixty-seven percent chance of survival, if you want to take a positive outlook on it. Thirty-three percent if you tend to be negative."

Click.

"Now we are getting down to the nitty-gritty, aren't we? Two shots left. You might want to think about that. Does the money mean that much to you?"

Davis looked at the gun. It looked like a poisonous viper, coiled and ready to strike. He stared at it, making no move to pick it up. "I know the percentages," he said, talking to the wall of the hotel room rather than to the man facing him. "You don't need to tell me."

The man shrugged, smiling.

Davis grabbed the gun. It felt as if it weighed a ton.

"You don't need to go through with it, you know. Your life is not worth the money," the man said.

Davis raised it with a quick motion and jammed it hard against his temple.

Click.

He nearly fainted. He did pee his pants. His first reaction was embarrassment, but then he didn't care if the man noticed or not. He was still alive. But then he realized he still had the gun pointed against the side of his head, frozen in place. The man did not ask for it back.

Davis slowly laid it back on the table, turning the handle toward the man. But the man did not reach for it. He sat perfectly still, his hands folded on his lap, looking at the gun.

Davis waited.

The man slowly reached out to move one stack of money next to other, pushing it towards Davis, then stood up to walk away. "Be sure to close the door when you leave," he said as he left the room.

Davis sat at the table for a long, long time, staring at the money and the gun. He finally reached over to take the two stacks of money.

He left the gun on the table. He carefully closed the door behind him.

Click.

Car Wash

TINA SENSED the two men were up to no good. They parked their battered Toyota Camry on the far edge of the lot, in the dark, away from the lights at the gas pumps. They sat for a long time, talking. They finally climbed out. One of the men approached the cashier's window while the other scurried into the obscurity at the end of the shed. Tina assumed he was positioning himself as the lookout for the holdup they were about to pull on her.

She had been afraid this was going to happen ever since she took this job. The car wash closed at six p.m. in the winter, and the gas pump business slowed to almost nothing an hour later. She was alone, stationed at the small window facing the pumps to accept payments for gas and to sell cigarettes, soda, candy, gum, motor oil, windshield wipers, and any other nickel-and-dime thing that the owner thought someone might purchase. The shed was locked and she was by herself, sitting on a stool behind the high counter next to the cash register in the brightly lit window. The owner wouldn't return until midnight to close up and take the cash receipts.

The job was boring, but even though her boyfriend complained about them, she loved the hours. She had the whole day to herself to get her two kids off to school,

"

nap a little, run errands, take care of things, and clean the apartment before picking up the kids in the afternoon to take them over to her mother to baby-sit them until she got home after work. But there was always the suppressed fear of being alone at night in a mini-convenience store/gas station. It was always there, in the back of her mind.

"Not very busy tonight, are you, hon?" the man said as he stepped up to the window.

"Busy enough," Tina replied nervously. "There is always a steady stream of cars coming in right up to when we close," she said, adding a small defensive white lie.

"That so? I heard you guys weren't very busy in the evening."

"Where'd you hear that?" Tina asked.

"Never mind," the man said.

"What can I do for you? You wanna pay for your gas before you pump?"

"No. Not really. I want a carton of Winstons and then all the money that you got in that there cash register."

Tina said nothing, frozen in the thought that her worst fear was actually happening. He was a big, mean, rough-looking man with a two-day stubble. He looked like he wouldn't worry much about hurting her.

She finally broke out of her fear to timidly tap the sign on the window that said the cash register never contained more than fifty dollars in the evenings. "You-you ain't going to get much," she said. "We have even less than that tonight. It ain't worth the effort."

"Don't bullshit me, girl," the man said, raising a gun to the window. Not pointing it at her, more like making sure she knew he had it. "Just do what I tell you, you hear?"

What she heard was someone banging on the door of the shed.

"Your friend ain't gonna get in, you know. That door is bolted and barred on the inside. Just for this kind of thing."

"I'm getting tired of talking to you, hon. I want this done before some asshole drives in here for gas."

Tina climbed off the stool to cross the small room to fetch a carton of Winstons. She placed the carton on the counter, then deliberately shoved it hard out the window, causing it to sail past the man's arm and bounce on the driveway. She used the instant of distraction to duck under the high counter. She scrunched up against the wall, out of sight, tucking her legs up tight. She was a small woman and knew he wouldn't be able to see her.

The man picked up the carton of cigarettes and came back to the window. "What the hell you doing?"

"Hiding."

"Get out from under there and give me the money!"

"I'm scared."

"You damn well should be."

"And I don't like you calling me 'hon' or 'girl.'"

"Do you like bitch any better?"

"I'm gonna call the cops."

"How you gonna do that? The phone is over there. I can see it. You reach for it and I'll cap your ass."

Tina looked across the room and realized he was right. She would be in the open if she tried to reach the phone, and she had no doubt he would shoot her. Even worse, her purse was sitting next to the phone. Her cell phone was in the purse. She was at a total loss about what to do, until she saw a long-handled mop propped in the corner. She inched over to grab it, then slowly stretched the long handle out to try to hook the strap of her purse.

"What the hell you doing now?"

"What does it look like?"

"Trying to find your cell phone in your purse?"

Tina didn't bother to answer, concentrating instead on sliding the heavy purse down the mop handle back to her under the counter. The man surprised her by shooting at the purse and the mop handle. He missed both, but Tina jumped at the sound of the shots and yelled, "Shit!" as she banged her head against the bottom of the counter, causing her to drop the mop and purse. She thought her eardrums were broken. She waited for a long moment for her heart to calm down, taking deep breaths, before daring to sweep her foot out to hook the purse strap with her toes. She was terrified that he was going to shoot her foot, but nothing happened.

"I hear you tapping on your cell phone, I'm gonna shoot right through this wall and kill you."

"I gotta gun in my purse," Tina said. Which was true. Her boyfriend gave it to her a month ago as a precaution for coming home late at night all by herself.

The man said, "Ah, shit," and Tina heard him walking away from the window. She heard his footsteps along the side of the shed, walking to where the other man was. She heard them talking but couldn't make out what they said.

The man came back to the window. "I'm gonna reach in and stretch over to open the cash register. You just stay down there and be quiet and we'll be outta here."

"If I hear you reaching across that counter, I will shoot up at you."

"What is your problem, bitch? It ain't your money."

"It ain't yours, either," Tina said.

"I need the money."

"And I need this job."

"It ain't worth being shot for."

"The money ain't worth going to jail for."

The man sighed. "Well, it don't matter none." She heard his weight leaning on the counter as he stretched in toward the cash register. She pulled the .38 Smith and Wesson out of her purse, cocked the hammer and fired up through the counter. Her boyfriend had told her that the .38 had a two-inch barrel, so it would fit in her purse. He said she probably couldn't hit anyone even if she aimed, but with a little luck, it might scare the hell out of somebody. She had never fired it before, and the noise and violence stunned her.

"Son of a bitch!" the man screamed.

"Go away!" Tina yelled.

The man shot a hole through the thin wooden wall, missing her head by inches. Tina thought her heart was going to come out through her mouth. She scrunched up even tighter, her heart pounding in terror, but she fired over her shoulder, back through the wall. She heard a metallic *plink* and shattering glass in the distance, across the parking lot.

"Damn, you just shot the side-view mirror off my car!"

If she wasn't so scared, she would have smiled in satisfaction.

"Who's gonna pay for that?"

"Call your insurance agent. Tell him that you were pulling a holdup and somebody shot the mirror off. I'll stand as a witness for that."

"You got a smart mouth, woman! And it's going to get you hurt!"

Tina was trembling too much to tap 911 on her cell phone. Instead she hit the speed dial button for her boyfriend. It rang and rang and rang with no response. She could also hear the second hold up man's cell phone ringing at the far end of the shed. She hung up quickly to see if she could hear what was being said on the phone outside. But his phone stopped ringing, too.

She tried her cell phone again. Again there was ringing outside the shed. The man with the gun yelled, "Answer your damn phone, Wilson, or turn it off."

Her boyfriend's voice came over her cell phone in a low, quiet whisper, "Tina?"

"Wilson?" Tina said, barely able to control herself. "Is that you out there by the shed door?"

"Yeah, it's me."

"What the hell do you think you are doing?"

"I need the money, Tina."

"Everybody seems to need the money tonight."

"Just give him the money and we're outta here."

"And then what happens next week when you need the money again? You gonna come back? The week after that, too? They're gonna get suspicious real quick, you know, if you hit this place every time I'm working. The cops ain't that stupid."

"It ain't like that, Tina. I promise."

Tina closed her eyes, nearly too tired to speak. "You're damn straight that it ain't like that! Your clothes and whatever else you got in my apartment better be out of there by the time I get home tonight. I never want to see your sorry ass again. And I'm bringing this gun home with me."

The man at the window was yelling, "She gonna give us the money or not, Wilson? She's your bitch, so make her get with it. You said she was going to roll over, and this was gonna be a piece of cake."

Tina threw the cell phone across the room and yelled out at the top of her voice, "Piss off, both of you!" then fired two more random shots through the front wall.

She heard the two men hurrying back to their car, the other man saying, "What in the hell is wrong with that woman?"

She stood up as she heard them drive off. She was tempted to take another shot. Instead she said to herself, "Goodbye, Wilson," crossing the room to dial 911.

The Viewing

MOMMA JOHNSON brushed imaginary dandruff from her son's shoulders and adjusted the knot of his tie, finally smoothing out the lapels of his jacket, as she had done a thousand times when he was alive. She then leaned over the casket to kiss him lightly on the forehead. It all felt so normal, so day-to-day, as if he was just taking a nap and would wake up in a few minutes to tell her he was going out and didn't know when he'd be back and not to wait up for him.

She sighed and stepped away from the dais, taking the last chair at the end of the front row so that everyone coming to the viewing could stop and talk to her as they came away from the casket. Her ankles were too swollen and her feet hurt too much for her to stand up for the next two hours to accept everybody's condolences. Her sister Stephanie, Jason's aunt, was already in the adjacent chair waiting for her. Stephanie was two years younger than Momma Johnson but almost as heavy.

"These folding chairs gonna bust my butt if we sit here too long," Stephanie said as Momma Johnson sat down.

"You can live with it. It ain't going to be that long," Momma Johnson replied, setting her overlarge shoulder bag on the floor next to her. It hit the floor with a clunk.

"What you got in that bag? A load of bricks?"

"Things," Momma Johnson said. "Things. A box of Kleenex, some hand wipes, some chocolate chip cookies, a Pepsi. Things I need to get me through this."

Aunt Stephanie patted her gently on the arm. "I know, Sweetie, I know. This ain't gonna be easy."

"It never is. You don't expect to outlive your children."

"Ain't that the truth."

Momma Johnson managed a sad smile and said, "But he is looking nice up there, ain't he? All dressed up. Nice suit. Shaved. His hair trimmed real nice."

"Fit to kill," Aunt Stephanie said, instantly regretting her words. Momma Johnson gave her a glance that let her know that those words would come back to haunt her at some future family argument. "The bullet wounds don't even show," Aunt Stephanie added lamely.

"The funeral home did a good job," Momma Johnson admitted. "Those evil boys blew away half his chest but they managed to reconstruct it. Looks normal, you know, up there in that casket."

Aunt Stephanie patted her arm one more time. Momma Johnson knew that the patting and squeezing were going to go on all night. It was going to be more than she could bear, but she knew she was just trying to be nice.

"He was a good boy," Stephanie said. "We all know that. He got into trouble now and then, but they all do that. That time in Juvie didn't hurt him, much."

Momma Johnson harrumphed in disagreement. "Those two years in Juvenile Home did him good. He learned a lot. Got some education. Made some friends. There are some good boys in there. Some good boys. Made some good contacts, too. It ain't like he joined a gang. More like he gained an extended family. Like that what-do-ya-call-it, like those war movies on HBO, you know?"

"Like 'A Band of Brothers'?" Aunt Stephanie asked.

"Yeah, that's it. Like a band of brothers."

"If you say so."

"I do. They had him working as soon as he got out. Making good money, too."

Aunt Stephanie knew she should back out on this, but she couldn't help herself. "Finally got him shot, didn't it?"

"Not by his friends. That was that other gang. Bunch of low-life dopers. They were trying to horn in on his territory. That just wasn't right. They will pay for it, too. You mark my words."

The two sisters did not have time discuss it further as the first guests started filing into the room, signing the visitors' book, then coming across to look at Jason. Some nodded sagely; some made the sign of the cross; others just stared wide-eyed at the dead boy, their hands in their pockets.

All of them finally came over to quietly console Momma Johnson and Aunt Stephanie. The older folks hugged the sisters; the really old folks shook their hands first, then hugged them. The younger people mostly mumbled a few words.

The commotion started while Momma Johnson was talking to old Mrs. Greer. She heard several chairs tipping over and saw people scattering to the back of the room. She turned to see a boy about Jason's age standing over the coffin, a gun in his hand. He looked down at Jason and shouted, "You miserable slime bucket! I ought to shoot you dead!"

Old Mrs. Greer backed away from Momma Johnson as if she had suddenly sprouted horns, then scurried out of the room as fast as her old legs could carry her. Momma Johnson and Aunt Stephanie froze on the spot, mesmerized by the boy waving the gun in the air. Momma Johnson finally found her voice and said, "He's already dead, boy. Can't you see that?"

"Not dead enough for me!"

"How much more dead can you be? There is no such thing as half dead."

Aunt Stephanie nudged her sister's shoulder to whisper, "I think the words are half pregnant. You can't be half pregnant. You can definitely be half dead. Happens all the time."

"I don't need your help on this," Momma Johnson hissed back.

The boy fired his pistol into the casket. The sound of the shot was deafening, and an acrid smell immediately choked everyone's throat. The boy waited for the sound to settle, then said, "How much more dead is that? That felt damned good."

"Stop that! You're ruining his good suit. Just stop that!" Momma Johnson shouted.

The boy looked at Momma Johnson and said, "Screw you!" and shot Jason two more times.

Momma Johnson was now jumping up and down in outrageous anger. "Don't you shoot him in the face! Don't you shoot him in the face! That would just ruin everything! I don't care about the suit, but don't shoot him in the face!" If her swollen ankles and sore feet didn't hurt so much, and if the boy didn't have a gun, she would have rushed up there to slap him along the side of the head.

The boy smiled when he heard Jason's mother yelling not to shoot him in the face. "Hell, I hadn't even thought of that," He pointed the gun at Jason's face, but a booming voice from the back of the room said, "Stop that, you fool!"

The boy looked up and said, "Who you calling a fool?"

"I'm calling you a fool."

The boy raised his gun and fired at the back of the room, shouting, "Screw you, too!"

The voice from the back of the room returned the shot, splintering the side of Jason's casket. Aunt Stephanie made an Olympian effort to wrestle Momma Johnson to the floor and pulled two metal folding chairs over them for protection.

"Let me up! Let me up!" Momma Johnson said, struggling against Stephanie's grip. "I gotta stop this nonsense. I paid good money for that casket. For that suit."

"Stay down! You could get shot!"

"They ain't shooting at me. They shooting at each other."

"Those bullets ain't got no name on 'em. They just kill anyone who is standing in front of them."

"I know those boys. They're friends of Jason. The one at the casket is Dejean Jones. And the one in the back is Leon Washington."

"They don't sound like friends of his right now," Stephanie said.

The voice in the back of the room yelled, "Drop your gun and get out, Dejean. You are disrespecting one of the brothers."

Dejean jerked off a shot, yelling back, "Like he didn't diss me? He took Jeanette, and when I called him on it, he told me to piss off."

"Who the hell is Jeanette?" Aunt Stephanie whispered.

"Cute little girl," Momma Johnson said. "She and Jason were all over each other. She called me to say she was coming tonight. I hope she doesn't walk through that door any minute now. That would be a mess."

"As if it ain't a mess now," Aunt Stephanie commented to no one in particular.

Another bullet whacked into the coffin. "Get out of here, Dejean."

That really pissed Momma Johnson off. She reached over for her oversized bag and fumbled out the contents, until a huge revolver thunked against the wooden floor.

"What the hell is that?" Aunt Stephanie asked. "It looks like a mobile cannon."

"Jason said it is a .357 Magnum. His gun. It's supposed to be able to blow off a barn door."

"What the hell you doing with it?

"I was going to hide it in the coffin after all of the people went home. I didn't know how in the hell else to get rid of it. I didn't want it in the house."

"If you go shoot that thing at either one of those dudes, you know they gonna shoot back at us and we ain't hiding behind anything but a couple of folding chairs."

Momma Johnson wrapped her hand around the enormous gun and said, "If I hit 'em, they ain't shooting back."

"You'd better use two hands. That is one big, dumb-ass gun."

Momma Johnson nodded and said, "Good idea." She gripped the gun with both hands to aim it at Dejean. The .357 Magnum exploded with a roar, knocking Momma Johnson back on her butt and taking out a huge chunk of the funeral home wall. Aunt Stephanie grabbed her ears in pain, knowing she was going to be hearing impaired for at least a month. Momma Johnson spun on her butt and fired another blast toward the back of the room, blowing a massive hole in the wooden door.

Dejean yelled, "Jesus!"

Leon Washington yelled, "Hey, I'm on your side, Momma Johnson!"

"I want both of you out of here, now!" Momma Johnson yelled back.

There was a long silence. Dejean finally said, "Don't fire that damn thing again. I'll go. But you gotta promise me not to shoot at me when I move away from this wooden box. That goes for you, too, Leon."

"I won't shoot if you get your sorry ass out of here. But you hesitate any longer or look back at Jason, I'll blow you a new asshole," Momma Johnson shouted.

"I won't shoot, either," Leon said.

Dejean made some fumbling noises from behind the casket, then took off in a dead sprint across the room and through the double side doors, apparently not keen on acquiring a second asshole.

After he was gone, Leon yelled, "I'm leaving, too, Momma Johnson."

"Wait a minute, Leon. Come and get this gun. The funeral director finds me with this damn thing, he gonna make me pay for all of the damages done in here, Stephanie and I will still be here when he comes. But if there ain't no guns, it ain't our fault for all the mess you two made."

Leon came down past the rows of chairs and took the gun, not saying anything. He was a good looking boy, about the same size as Jason but a little older. He walked out the back door casually as if nothing had happened.

Momma Johnson pulled herself up, with the help of Aunt Stephanie, and flopped onto one of the chairs. "See if you can find any of them chocolate chip cookies in my bag."

Aunt Stephanie reached over to pick up the bag and slumped down next to Momma Johnson. "All of that over a girl? Can you imagine? We never had any shootouts over us when we was young. That would have been something, wouldn't it?"

Momma Johnson stared at the hole she had blown into the far wall then said wistfully, "Yeah, that would have been something."

Bank Job

MATTHEW CALLED IT positive visualization. He pictured the robbery step by step, reviewing the sequence in his mind's eye. He tried to imagine every possible detail of what might (or might not) happen once he was inside the bank. A timid man, the thought of daring to rob a bank in the middle of the day was overwhelming. But he prodded himself forward by remembering the old joke about the embarrassed robber: The guy rehearses each step continually, day after day, in order not to make a mistake but then, on the day of the performance, he pulls out his gun and yells, "All right, you stickers, this is a fuck-up!"

That was not going to happen to him. If he could help it.

The scenario was simple: He would walk into the bank, stand in line, wait patiently until he arrived at the counter, then hand over the written note that announced: *This is a robbery. I have a gun. Fill up the sack I am handing to you. Do not hit the silent alarm. No exploding ink in the money or I will come back and harm you.*

He would then take back the bag, now filled with money, and walk casually out of the bank. He would not run, because that might draw attention to himself.

Once outside the bank, he would slip into the adjacent alley to pull off the hooded sweatshirt, dump the sun glasses and the knit hat into the trash bin, so he would look entirely different from the robber recorded on the security cameras. Then he would just walk away. Piece of cake. Nothing to it.

Reality intruded.

There were no waiting lines in front of the counter. His intent had been to compose himself while standing behind the other customers, to mentally rehearse everything one more time. Instead he found himself walking straight to the counter to immediately face the teller.

"May I help you, sir?" the young woman asked in a pleasant voice.

Matthew stared at her for a moment, startled by how cute she was. She looked like that actress in all of those silly romance movies–thin, short blond hair, dimples, a light tan (*artificial?*) that contrasted beautifully with her white blouse. The acrylic name plaque on the counter said Ashley. Then he remembered his note. He couldn't find it. He desperately searched through his pockets, too embarrassed to look at the young woman. He finally dug it out of the pouch of his hooded sweatshirt. He fumbled it when he handed it to her and didn't get a chance to unfold it. She frowned, but accepted it with a fleeting (*false?*) smile, opening it slowly.

Her face broke into a large grin.

She leaned across the counter to whisper to him, "This is so exciting. This has never happened to me before."

In spite of himself, Matthew leaned forward to whisper back, "How long have you been working here?"

"Two weeks. I was trained for this just last week."

"Well, don't do anything stupid."

"That's what they said in training, 'Don't do anything stupid,' so you must be good at this. How many banks have you robbed?"

"This is my first."

"Oh, this is so cool."

Matthew sighed. He could feel his blood pressure mounting. This was taking longer than he liked. "Look, we should probably move along, if you don't mind."

"Did you see that old Woody Allen movie where the bank robber hands the teller the note and she can't read it? She reads, 'I have a gub' and then says 'What's a gub?' Then Woody Allen has to explain it. That was so funny. But your handwriting is good. Very good. Great cursive. Very rare these days."

Matthew reminded her, "Do you mind? I really want to get this over with."

"Oh, sure. Give me your bag or whatever."

Matthew pulled out the bag wedged under his belt to hand it across the counter.

"A Walmart bag? You're robbing the bank with a Walmart bag? Couldn't you find something else? Like a black money bag or something?"

"This is all I had at home," Matthew said, trying hard to keep his voice down.

"This is really tacky."

"Just get on with it, please."

Without glancing at the tellers on either side of her, Ashley began to fill the Walmart bag with the money from her till. But she glanced up when she heard the racking noise of a shotgun being cocked and saw a man in a ski mask standing in the middle of the bank lobby with the shotgun pointed at the ceiling. "Oh my," she said quietly to Matthew. "This could get complicated."

As Matthew looked around, the man in the ski mask announced loudly, "This is a bank robbery. I want everyone to step out from behind their desks and from behind their counters and I want everyone down on the floor, out here in the center of the lobby, down on the floor. If you move quickly, no one will be hurt."

Ashley handed Matthew his Walmart bag, filled with money. She muttered, "You had better take this now or you're going to lose out. That wouldn't be fair. You were here first. Maybe you should hide it under your sweat-shirt."

Matthew nodded, doing as he was told, but whispered back, "Hit the silent alarm before you come around."

"What? Oh, right."

Matthew laid face down on the center of the lobby floor as the few other bank customers were doing. The bank employees were coming around their desks and the counter to join them. A couple of the women, including Ashley, climbed over the top of the counter to drop to the floor. Ashley hiked her skirt up as she came across the counter, and Matthew knew he shouldn't be looking, but he did anyway, and liked what he saw. He was pleased when she flopped down beside him.

The man in the ski mask stopped two of the tellers to hand them two large duffel bags, directing one to clean out the tills behind the counter, and the other to go to the safe. He admonished them to hurry, waving the shotgun around in jerky wide arcs.

"Did you see those bags?" Ashley said into Matthew's ear. "Those are good bags. You need something like that."

"Maybe next time," Matthew hissed back, wishing she would shut the hell up.

"Take your gun out and shoot him."

"I don't have a gun."

"Your note said you had a gun."

"My note *insinuated* I had a gun."

"Insinuated? Excuse me? It said you had a gun. I read it."

"I didn't want anybody to get hurt."

The man in the ski mask walked over and kicked Matthew hard in the hip, shouting, "I want you two love birds to shut up, you hear me?"

Matthew yelled, *"Owww,"* and grabbed at his hip to massage the pain, nodding to the man that he was definitely, definitely, going to shut up. The man walked away from them to supervise the two tellers with his duffel bags.

"You okay?"

"Shut up," Matthew whispered as forcefully as he could.

"Don't get mad at me. I didn't kick you."

From that point on, things happened fast. Cop sirens came screaming around the street corner outside the bank, and the robber panicked and dropped his gun. He grabbed the bags from the two tellers and ran out the side door instead of the front door. There was shouting and running on the sidewalk just as three cops came through the front door with their guns out, yelling, "Stay down. Nobody move. Stay down."

Ashley whispered, "Give me your bag."

"What?"

"Give me your bag. You're never going to make it out of here with it."

"You going to turn me in?"

"Don't be stupid. I can hide it here, and then bring it to you after I'm off work."

"But . . ."

"The money from the till is already gone. The bank won't know the difference. They'll assume the robber took it along with all the other cash he's taken. It will take them a while to sort that out. And nobody's going to think about the top of an old Walmart bag sticking out of my big purse."

The cops were still walking around, looking and sounding officious, pulling the bank manager and the bank guards to their feet, but still yelling for everyone else to stay down.

Matthew carefully slipped the Walmart bag from under his sweatshirt to slide it over to Ashley. She took the bag and slid it under her body, knotting the top so none of the bills would slip out.

"Where do I meet you? When?"

"The Starbucks. Around the corner. Six p.m."

"How do I know I can trust you?"

She gave him a smile that melted his heart, but said, "You don't."

Matthew sighed and stood up when the cops told them to do so.

He followed their instructions and joined the small groups that were to go to different corners of the bank so they could be interrogated. The bank employees and tellers went back to their posts. He looked back at Ashley, but she was busy behind her counter, putting things in order.

As planned, he later walked around to the alley to dump his knit hat, sweatshirt and sunglasses into the dumpster, then wandered around town the rest of the afternoon, aimlessly killing time until six o'clock.

He entered Starbucks a half hour early and stood in the crowd, scanning the board to find a drink he could afford. Two-dollar cups of coffee were not on the menu. He wondered how much he (and Ashley) had stolen. Maybe they could at least afford a café latté, each.

But she never showed.

He fidgeted, but sat at a table to watch out the window until he thought he might vomit, expecting the cops to come crashing through the front door any second, certain that Ashley had ratted on him. Or maybe she had been caught with the money. He could feel it. They had arrested her. They accused her of being an accomplice. She had rolled over. They identified him from the security cameras. They saw them together on the cameras whispering to each other, huddled together on the floor. She was going to rat on him to save herself. She would bring them here. What had he done to her? What had he done to himself?

He left, hoping no one had noticed him sitting there for an hour.

In spite of himself, he stood at the door when the bank opened in the morning. His best white polo shirt, Docker slacks, Sperry loafers, a preppy coming in to count his money. No way anyone could relate him to the security cameras from the day before. No way.

Ashley was not at the counter.

He walked to where her position had been. An elderly woman, old enough to be his mother, smiled at him. "I-is Ashley here today?" he asked.

"Ashley? Oh, no. The poor thing. She was a nervous wreck after that . . . incident . . . yesterday. It terrified her. She quit. Just like that. Said she couldn't handle such stress. Said she would never be comfortable working here after that. I don't blame her, poor thing."

"D-do you have her address? Or phone number? I-I'm a friend of hers."

"Oh, we can't give that kind of thing out to our customers. It wouldn't be right. You know that."

Matthew turned away, almost in tears. But he wasn't sure if it was for the money or because he would never see Ashley again.

But another woman, more Ashley's age, tapped him on the shoulder before he exited the bank. "Sorry, but is your name Gub?"

"Gub?"

"Yes. Ashley told me that a good-looking young man might come in asking about her. I heard you talking to Mrs. Quinn at the counter. Ashley said I should ask the young man if he was Gub."

"Gub? Oh, yeah, right, Gub. I'm Gub."

The woman handed him an envelope. He took it and continued to walk out the door. The envelope and the note smelled of perfume. Her handwriting was neat, almost artistic.

Gub, I am truly sorry about this. It was a lot of money and I needed it badly. I can find another job, but I really needed this extra money now. Better luck on your next job. XOXO, Ashley.

Carjacking

JACKSON AND LESHAWNE were in an ugly mood. No one would give them a ride to the mall. They finally had to take the Metro bus, slouching low in the seats so no one could see them. The massive parking lot in the hot sun turned their mood from ugly to surly as they looked in vain for a vehicle to 'jack, like something slick and sleek that would impress their homeys.

Then they thought they had it: A dude walked out of Macy's, going straight for a black Dodge Viper. Definitely a sweet ride—but their timing was off. The dude blew out of his parking space before they could get there, laying a strip of rubber and blue smoke all the way to the exit. Jackson and LeShawne were outraged. They didn't get the license plate number, but they agreed the next time they saw a black Dodge Viper, the driver was in trouble. The car was gonna be theirs for sure, and they were gonna trash his ass, too, as payback.

They went once more around the parking lot, in the hot sun, righteously pissed. Have a good day, your ass. By mutual but unspoken understanding, they were not doing any more sports cars. Gonna go instead for something big. Something oversized. Something that would take up space in the 'hood. Something they could party in.

And there it was—a Chevrolet Suburban. Huge sucker. As long as a van but flashy like an SUV. Three rows of seats on the inside. They could get wasted in there; smoking, drinking, playing with the sisters, trashing the interior, remembering it tomorrow as a truly great night.

Gotta have a plan: Retreat to the shade at the side of the mall, wait for as long as it takes, and take shit from nobody.

The wait wasn't long. They didn't see where she came from, but one of the side doors opened and shut, then a woman walked around to stuff packages in the back. Jackson and LeShawne barely reacted in time. She was almost to the driver's door before they intercepted her.

Jackson motioned for LeShawne to take the right side while he sprinted around the left to grab the woman. If Jackson was too slow, LeShawne would jump in the passenger side to push her back out. But Jackson caught up to her just as she was climbing up behind the steering wheel.

He grabbed her by her shirt collar to yank her out. Good looking white woman. Fairly young. Short blond hair, white dress shirt, blue jeans, Nikes without socks. Her eyes went wide in panic.

She had nothing in her hands. Her purse was probably in the seat. Jackson yanked the silver watch from her wrist, then gave her a vicious shove, saying, "Beat it, bitch!" slamming her hard against the adjacent car.

He swung up into the seat with an easy athletic grace. The keys were in the ignition. LeShawne was already in the passenger seat yelling, "Go! Go! Go!"

They blasted backward out of the parking space, whipped around toward the exit, laying rubber just like the black Dodge Viper, only slower, already laughing at how good they were. LeShawne looked back and reported, "Oh man, that woman is pissed. Really pissed. She's waving her hands and yelling at us. Now she just pulled her cell phone from her jeans pocket and is hitting the numbers."

"Calling 911," Jackson said, then slipped into a mimicking female voice, "Oh, officer, officer, my car has been stolen. My precious Chevrolet Suburban has been stolen. Please help me."

Then they heard a phone ringing in the back seat.

"What the hell is that? The stupid broad's calling her own car?"

"No. It's mine," a timid voice said from the back seat.

Jackson and LeShawne both looked around to see a small boy hiding low behind the seats.

"How did you get in here?" Jackson asked.

"I-I climbed in, before you grabbed Momma."

"I didn't see you getting into the car."

The boy just shrugged.

"How old are you?"

"Ten. But I will be eleven next month."

"Shit!"

"Can I answer my phone? It's Momma."

"Give me the goddamn phone. I'll talk to Momma!" LeShawne said, reaching back to grab the phone from the kid. He turned to Jackson to ask, "What we gonna do? This is freaking kidnapping. Carjacking is no big deal, but kidnapping a kid? They'll get their nose all out of joint about that!"

Jackson nodded. "Dump him out. Give him back his phone so his momma can find him or call her back yourself and tell her he's at Fulton and 10th and she should come get her goddamned kid."

"I can't find Herman," the kid said.

Both Jackson and LeShawne glanced back at the kid.

"Your baby brother's here, too?" Jackson asked.

"I don't have a baby brother."

"So who the hell is Herman?"

"My snake."

Jackson smashed on the brakes, fish-tailing the Suburban, almost getting hit by a Ford Taurus behind them.

"You got a snake in this car? You got a loose snake in this car?"

"His box tipped over when you were taking those hard turns at the mall."

"What kinda snake is it?" LeShawne asked.

"Who gives a fuck what kinda snake it is! It's a snake!" Jackson shouted, slowly edging back into traffic.

But LeShawne had more questions. "How big is it? Does it bite?" He raised his feet off the floor to plant them high up on the dashboard. Jackson noticed the gesture and was very conscious of having his feet on the pedals, with nowhere else to put them, thinking that he should make dumb ass LeShawne do the driving.

"Six feet. But he only bites when he is upset. Then he gets real mean."

"Six-freaking-feet? That's taller than I am! How do you know when he's upset?'

"He gets upset when there is a lot of noise and shouting."

"Like now?"

The boy nodded and repeated, "Like now."

"Why can't you find him?" Jackson asked, frantically looking around at the back. "He's six-freaking-feet. Ain't he laying on the floor or the seat?"

"No. He does this all the time. He finds a hole and climbs into the seats or the side panels to hide. Then he wiggles from one seat to another or climbs into the vents and comes out somewhere else. He does that at home, too, hiding in the sofas and heating vents."

"Shit," LeShawne said.

"Momma hates it when he does that."

"No shit."

"Screw this. Do something, LeShawne," Jackson ordered.

"And just what the fuck it is that you want me do, big man? Climb around the freaking seats looking for a freaking six-foot snake? Pull my freaking gun out and shoot through the freaking seats or into the freaking side panels and hope that I hit him? Or maybe we dump the kid and drive off and look for the snake later tonight, just to be sure I got him? And who is going to pull the freaking snake out? You or me?

"Oh, man, I've had enough of this shit," LeShawne continued. "Just pull over and let me out. *Now*. Then you and the kid can deal with Mr. Herman, the six-foot-hidden-I-don't-know-what-kind-of-pissed-off-snake it is. I'm outta here."

Jackson pulled over to the curb, and they both got out, not bothering to turn off the engine, slamming the doors hard in disgust.

Timothy watched them walk away, yelling at each other, gesturing wildly, occasionally punching each other on the shoulder. He waited to be sure they were not coming back before he dialed Momma. He knew she would be scared and he was afraid they had hurt her when they pushed her away from the car like that. He would just tell her they got angry when they found him in the car and decided to leave him alone and went away.

He wasn't going to tell her about making up the story about the snake in the car. She always got angry with him when he made up stories like that.

The Bridge

DUANE STOPPED a few yards from the woman and leaned forward to rest his forearms on the bridge railing. She did not acknowledge him.

"You gonna jump?" he asked.

No response.

He took a quarter from his jeans and flipped it out and away from the bridge. It tumbled over and over for a long time before hitting the water. "Damn," he said.

She remained frozen in place, on the outside of the railing, one hand grasping the rail, the other hand clutching a small black purse. Her breath puffed out against the cold night air. Her red cloth coat looked too thin for this weather. But she fit neatly on the ledge, her heels parked tight against the balustrade, her toes protruding just slightly over the void. Black pumps. A nice match to the red coat and black purse. The blond ponytail was also held together by a black ribbon. A desperate, chic chick.

"That's a long way down," Duane said, "Gonna be a thrill, like a bungee jump without the happy ending. From this height the water is going to feel like a brick wall. You're gonna break something, you know? Maybe you should dive, like head first, to make sure you do it right, break your neck straight away. Water's gonna be cold, too."

"Leave me alone," she snapped, finally turning her head to look at him.

"Don't get mad at me. I ain't making you jump. I just stopped to watch."

"Go away."

He smiled at her. "It's a free bridge. You can jump. I can watch."

She returned to her impersonation of a statue.

"Can I ask you a question?"

She held her head rigidly forward this time, locked in place. "I don't want to talk about it."

"That wasn't my question."

She spoke again without looking at him, staring into the dark space in front of her. "What's your question?"

"If you're gonna jump, do you need your purse?"

She looked at her purse as if surprised she still had it. "I-I didn't realize I was still holding it," she said softly.

"You got any money in it? Credit cards?"

She turned this time to give him an angry glare. "I'm jumping off the bridge and you're trying to mug me?"

Duane held his hands out, offended. "I'm not trying to mug you, for chrissakes. I'm panhandling. The second you step off the bridge, you no longer need your purse. I could use any money you might have in there. You're just going to get it all wet and probably ruin it. And if you have a couple of credit cards, I can use them tonight and maybe again tomorrow morning before anyone realizes you're missing. It's not like you're gonna worry about paying the bills."

"Go to hell."

"You may make it there before I do," he replied

Angry silence.

"I'll make you a deal. If you have a cell phone or any ID in your purse, I'll call whoever you want and tell them you took the plunge."

She inched farther away, gripping the purse even tighter. "If you're that hard up for money, maybe you should jump, instead of me."

"I'm hard up, lady, not stupid. Plus I'm afraid of heights and I hate cold water."

She sighed. "If I give you money, will you go away and leave me alone?"

"What the hell you hanging on to the purse for? You think you need an ID to get into heaven? Somebody's going to card you at the gates? How about this for a deal? You give me the purse and I'll give you a push. Then you don't have to stand here all night freezing your ass off."

She scooted even farther away, using short, dragging steps as if afraid she might trip and fall off the ledge. Duane thought about pointing that out to her, but she caught him by surprise by carefully sinking down to position the purse on the ledge next to her feet. "Come and get it if you want it that badly." She again edged away a few more inches.

Duane blinked, not sure what to say, "Y-you want me to call someone for you? After you jump, I mean?"

"Do what you damn please."

He started to crawl over the railing to fetch the bag but had second thoughts. It was too scary out there, on the other side. Instead, he walked along the railing to where the purse was and tried to stretch over the railing to reach for it. But it was too far. So he crawled on top of the railing, balancing on his belly, his legs dangling above the bridge floor, stretching his arm out as far as he could.

He was stunned to feel her hands on the collar of his coat and the back of his belt. She was pulling him over the railing. He scrabbled for a hold with one hand and grabbed at her with the other. But she was too fast, too strong. He found himself tumbling over and over, for a long time, before hitting the cold, hard water.

The woman bent over to pick up the purse, not bothering to look down at the river. In any event, Duane was already gone.

"Annoying bastard," she said to herself as she hiked up her skirt and coat to climb back over to the inside of the bridge, adding, "But at least he made me feel better!"

Initiation Night

"STOP DICKING WITH the damn gun," Rasheed said. Jason sat next to him on the front seat, playing with the cheap .38 Smith & Wesson. He was flipping the gun's cylinder in and out, then spinning it. *Flip. Spin. Spin. Flip. Spin. Spin.* "You're going to fuck up and shoot your stupid balls off. That gun don't have no safety." Truth was, Rasheed was less worried about Jason shooting his balls off than he was about getting the gun back in one piece. He had lent it to Jason when they had gotten into the car and was now sorry he had.

Jason responded by giving him the glare, the acquired prison *don't-fuck-with-me* glare that was supposed to put people in their place, but Jason had never been in prison (yet) and he was only 14 years old and still cursed with baby cheeks, soft blue eyes and smooth skin. The glare came off as a teenage pout that didn't intimidate his own baby sister back in the 'hood. They were cruising down Lincoln Boulevard, waiting for a sucker to flick his lights at them.

Jerome was in the back seat, saying nothing but looking mean and menacing. Sitting next to him was Washington, Jason's cousin, who was smoking what he said was weed but smelled like wet hay. But it worked for him. He was giggling and talking to himself and only now and then focusing on what was going on around him, which at this moment caused him to repeat, "Shoot your stupid balls off," leading him into another giggling fit, which told Jason that he was not going to get much backup from his cousin tonight, no matter what happened.

Rasheed continued to drive, irritated at all of them. They were not respecting his vehicle. He felt someone should compliment him on such a sweet ride, on the comfort and the sound system of this slick, dark green Lincoln Navigator SUV. He had boosted it on the street last night and liked it so much that he had even gone over to New Jersey to switch some plates from another car, to confuse the cops for a day or two, at least.

The plan for tonight was simple: They would drive around until some jerk flicked his lights at them in a well-meaning effort to tell them that they were driving without their lights on. They would then turn and follow him until Rasheed could corner the sucker with the SUV. Jason would earn his bones by jumping out of the SUV to shoot the unlucky driver in the head.

After that they would celebrate with a few beers, maybe smoke some of that cheap hay that Washington was inhaling, then take Jason downtown to get the tattoo on the forearm of the devil's head with bleeding fangs and KD underneath, and then finally find some sisters to get him laid, making him one of them, a man and a full member of the righteously feared Kill Devil gang.

The wait wasn't long. They had barely gone four blocks when a blue Ford Taurus coming across the intersection flicked its lights, twice, as if angry at them for driving around without their lights on.

Rasheed didn't say a word. He cranked the SUV around into a tight U-turn in the middle of the intersection, ignoring the cars honking at them, hurrying to catch up to the Taurus.

"You gonna do this, Jason?" Jerome asked in an intimidating voice that would not accept no as an answer.

"He's gonna do it," Rasheed said, impatient now, not taking his eyes off the Taurus a few cars in front of him.

"*Heh, heh, heh,* my cuz Jason is going to do this, ain't you, Cuz?" Washington giggled.

Jason spun the .38's cylinder. *Spin. Spin. Spin.* Staring at the Taurus.

"I'm gonna pass him and cut him off at the next intersection," Rasheed warned, pulling the SUV out into the left lane.

But as they passed the Taurus, Jason said, "Oh, shit, it's a woman!"

Jerome sneered, "So?"

"I thought it was gonna be a dude, not some old white woman!"

"Who gives a fuck?"

"Shoot your stupid balls off, *heh, heh, heh,*" Washington giggled.

"She looks like one of the teachers over at the middle school!"

"Cut her off, Rasheed," Jerome ordered.

Rasheed swerved far left, then cut back hard to the right to stop perpendicular in front of the Taurus, T-boning her to a stop. There was a screech of brakes and an angry horn.

"This ain't right. It oughta be some dude."

"Just shut up and do it, Jason. Now!"

Jason shrugged, expressing his indifference, and opened the door to step down from the passenger seat of the SUV, holding the .38 straight out with both hands.

Then nothing went as expected.

The woman behind the wheel didn't flinch, didn't shield herself with her hands, nor try to back her car away. Instead she stomped on the accelerator and rocketed the Taurus forward, directly at Jason, who barely managed to leap out of the way before the car smashed into the side of the SUV, exactly at the spot where he had been standing.

Jason tripped as he jumped out the way and fell hard onto the street. He quickly scrambled to his feet, feeling dazed, and watched in wonder as the woman backed up, suddenly realizing that she was coming at him again. He dove back through the open door to the perceived safety of the passenger seat of the SUV. The Lincoln rocked violently a split second later as the Taurus slammed back into its side.

"What the fuck is going on?" Rasheed screamed.

"She's trying to kill me!" Jason screamed back.

Jerome cursed, "That dumb bitch!"

"Jesus, she's coming again!" Washington shouted, joining the others in reality. The SUV rocked a third time before he could finish the sentence.

"She's destroying my car!" Rasheed shouted.

"That woman has some anger problems," Washington said.

"Turn around and get out of here," Jerome ordered.

"Where's my gun?" Washington asked, fumbling through his baggy clothes. "I'll show her. Where's my fucking gun?"

Rasheed tried to reverse the SUV to straighten it into the street but Jason was climbing on top of the gear console trying to get away from the bashing of the Ford Taurus. Jerome was shouting, "Move, move, move!" while Washington found his gun, But he pulled it out too hard and accidentally squeezed the trigger, blowing a hole through the roof, causing everyone in the car to grab their ears from the blast.

"Oh, shit, sorry, sorry," he muttered.

Rasheed managed to push Jason off the gear console and straightened the SUV, but the woman rammed him from behind before he could get started.

"I've had enough of this shit," Jerome said, pulling out his own gun and firing over the back seat through the SUV, blowing out the rear window. But the SUV was so much higher that it passed harmlessly over the Taurus' roof.

"Oh, man, my car, my car," Rasheed whined.

The woman rammed the rear once again, jolting them hard.

"Stop the car," Jerome said, his voice evil incarnate. He opened the door and stepped down to directly face the Taurus, his gun in his hand. But the woman swerved around the SUV, slam banging the side of both cars as she went straight for him. He jumped back into the SUV just as she tore off its door at high speed.

Washington was waving his gun around, yelling, "Oh, shit, oh, shit," then aimed it out the side door that no longer existed and fired again.

"Oh. *Ow. Ow. Ow.* You just shot me in the fucking foot, you sorry son of a bitch!" Jerome yelled.

"Oh shit, man. Sorry. Sorry."

The Taurus stopped a hundred feet in front of the SUV.

"Now what is she doing?" Rasheed asked in utter amazement.

Jason peeked over the dashboard and saw smoke spinning off the Taurus' rear tires. "She's going to ram us with her trunk," he said, totally impressed. "I saw this on ESPN. The Demolition Derby. She's gonna smash in our radiator so we can't drive no more!"

"Where's my gun?" Rasheed shouted at Jason. "Shoot the bitch while she's in front of us!"

"I don't have it! I don't have it! I musta dropped it in the street when she tried to run over me!"

And the Taurus smashed full speed into them, crumpling the trunk of the Taurus but shoving the SUV's radiator back into its engine compartment. The Lincoln Navigator died in a hiss of steam and a grinding of metal as the woman pulled away. She again stopped a hundred feet in front of them and started spinning her wheels for another backward bash. Jason was hiding under the dashboard, fumbling with his cell phone. Rasheed was holding his broken wrist to fight back against the pain but managed to ask, "Who the hell you calling?"

"The cops. Before the dumb bitch kills us."

The cops were already arriving on the scene, and it didn't take them long to sort out the situation. The four men from the SUV were taken into custody, two of them in an ambulance. Later, when both vehicles were pulled over to the side of the road, with cops kicking debris off the street surface and waving cars past the flashing squad cars, one of the older cops wrapped a blanket around the shoulders of the woman and handed her cup of coffee. "Why did you do that, Mrs. McAndrew?" he said. "That was an extraordinarily dangerous thing to do."

Mrs. McAndrew did not respond for a long moment, as if searching for the words to explain it, but then glanced at the forearm of the older cop and smiled when she saw the USMC tattoo.

"What was the first thing the Marines taught you to do when caught in an ambush?"

The older cop hesitated, puzzled by the strange question, then said, "Attack. Don't try to run away, because you would drop your defense and there may be other ambushers behind you or to another side of you. And most ambushers do not expect you to attack into the ambush, so you have the element of surprise, taking theirs away. That's Marine Corps doctrine. But what has that got to do with this?"

Mrs. McAndrew let the blanket slide off her shoulders, lifting the short sleeve of her blouse to show him the shoulder tattoo with its globe and anchor and the letters USMC.

"Semper fi, Mac."

Convenience Store

PATEL FELT SOMETHING was wrong when the two men walked into the convenience store. One wore a crocheted stocking cap that was inappropriate for the summer night and the other had a black do rag that made him look mean. Both looked nervous. They fooled around the magazine rack before picking up a box of donuts, then took a long time to come up to the counter.

"Anything else?" Patel asked.

"Carton of Marlboros," the first man said.

The second one pulled out a gun, giggling as if embarrassed to have a gun in his hand but added, "And all of the money you got in the cash register, bro." He didn't point the gun at Patel, just held it down alongside his leg.

"You know there isn't much money in there," Patel said, his voice a little high, trying to stay calm. "Fifty dollars, not more. It's been a slow night."

"You're lying, bro. We seen people coming in and out all night."

Patel shrugged. "Ain't my money and I sure as hell don't want to get shot over it, but it's been nickel and dime all night. I just don't want you to be disappointed. It ain't worth an armed robbery charge."

The man in the crocheted cap made a face and reached under his T-shirt to pull out his own gun. "Let us worry about that."

Patel nodded and said, "You got it," and hit the release button on the cash register. But the entry bell to the front door jingled again. All three men turned to stare at two other men walking into the store.

"Dammit, I told you to lock the door after we came in," Crocheted Cap whispered to Do Rag.

"You didn't tell me shit," Do Rag whispered back.

Patel raised his hands off the cash register and asked, "What do you want me to do?"

"Close the register and then we gonna step back over there, behind that aisle, and wait. You take their money and then get them the fuck out of here. And remember, we got guns."

"Like I'd forget."

"Don't be smart, boy!"

Patel shrugged and shut the cash register. Crocheted Cap and Do Rag stepped around the aisle just as the other two men walked up to the counter.

Patel managed to control his voice. "May I help you?"

"A carton of Marlboros."

"And all of the money you got in the cash register."

"I, uh, I think you might want to talk to those two guys."

"Talk to who?"

"To us, motherfucker."

"Who the hell . . ." But the man stopped when he saw the two guns coming around the aisle.

The man behind him pulled a gun from under his T-shirt and said, "I'm gonna cap your asses, motherfuckers."

Patel ducked under the counter just as at least two guns went off. The sound was stunning, and a choking acrid smell instantly filled the small store. Apparently no one was hurt, as no one yelled or screamed or fell down and there were sounds of feet scrambling away in opposite directions to hide behind different aisles.

"We were here first, you stupid mofos."

"Big fucking deal."

Someone fired again, and there was a crash of glass in the frozen food section, which prompted someone to shoot back, causing a crash of glass at the front door.

"The man behind the counter says there ain't but fifty dollars in the till."

"Well, it's our fifty dollars, asshole."

"Then step right up and get it, dumb shit. It will be the last fifty dollars you will ever see."

"We got all night and probably a lot more ammunition than you got!"

There was a long silence as both sides glanced at their watches and counted their bullets.

"Fifty dollars? We could split it four ways. Twenty-five dollars each."

"What are you? One of them dumb shits that got left behind?"

That merited another shot, which splattered a five pound sack of Gold Medal flour.

"You'd better not be trying to outflank us, 'cause we're watching for it."

"Keep watching, asshole."

Suddenly there were sirens off in the distance, but it was difficult to tell if they were coming toward the store or not.

"You'd better not have called the cops, boy, or all four of us will cap your white ass."

Silence.

"You hear me, boy?"

"Asshole probably fainted."

The sirens were coming closer.

"Somebody's going to have to make a move here!"

Silence, then, "Okay, don't shoot at us. We're gonna back outta the front door. You can have the money and the fucking cops, too!"

"I'll shoot at you if I want to shoot at you," Crocheted Cap yelled, but he couldn't see the other men go out the front door, because they crouched low and used the aisles to cover themselves until the entry bell jingled to tell everyone they were out the door and gone.

Do Rag started after them, but Crocheted Cap grabbed his arm to hold him back. "They may be waiting out there for us, bro. We'll grab the money and go out the back door."

They crept around the counter, expecting to see Patel huddled in fear on the floor, probably peeing his pants. But he was not there. And the cash register was open and empty. And the back door was open. Crocheted Cap and Do Rag stared at each other, just starting to understand what happened and to get pissed about it, when the cops came busting through both the front and back doors, yelling at them. "Drop your guns and get down! Get down!"

The newspaper reported the next day that two men had been arrested and another two were still being sought. It also reported that nearly $200 was taken from the cash register. Patel Diol, who was working in the store when the robbery took place, was quoted as saying he had no idea which pair took it.

Sisters

I DID IT. I will admit I did, if they ever catch me. But I had to protect her from him. He was cheating on her, abusing her, making her look like a weak, defenseless fool. I couldn't let that go on any longer.

It didn't start that way.

In the beginning they were a beautiful couple. She was the valedictorian at Vassar and he, the first in his class, the Brigade Commander, at West Point. My older sister, so bright, so lovely, so talented, married to the First Captain at the Academy, walking out of the chapel under an arch of swords. At that moment I loved him, too. Maybe as much as she did, though I never told anyone.

Coming down the stairs to drive off for their honeymoon, William laughed when he saw me and kissed me on the cheek, close to my lips, and said quietly, just to me, "Maybe I married the wrong sister." He was so handsome in his uniform with all those bright buttons and ribbons and stiff collar and rakish shoulder patches, I almost fainted.

I remembered that kiss the rest of my life. The warmth, the tenderness, next to my lips. And the words.

They started so well after that. The Army shuttled William off to Fort Benning for training and then a bunch of other schools, while Agatha went for her master's at Georgetown.

I did not start that well. I flunked out of NYU, living on Adderall, then living *for* Adderall. At first it kept me focused, until I could focus only on Adderall. But I couldn't go home. Too embarrassed. I didn't tell our parents. And Agatha did not tell them either. I stayed in the city, waiting tables, selling perfumes and makeup in department stores, pushing lattés at Starbucks, cleaning hotel rooms. Getting by. Just getting by. As long as I could fool another doctor into writing me a prescription.

William volunteered for Iraq, and Agatha got an internship in D.C., while I ran out of sources for my scripts. My workmates knew who I was (or I should I say, what I was?) and introduced me to better things, cheaper than Adderall. Things that came without a script.

William came back after his tour to work in the Pentagon, and Agatha had a baby, a boy, Billy, and they were both so happy. Agatha sent me photos from her phone. I lost my dingy apartment in New York and found a squat uptown. William went back to Iraq.

I moved in with Joe. He dealt. I lost my jobs. But I kept Joe happy.

Agatha was pregnant again but lost this baby and asked me to come down to D.C. to live with her while William was gone. But I didn't know if I could, because I didn't know anybody there and I had never been honest with Agatha about my feelings for William. But Joe called me a freaking skank and didn't want me around anymore, so I caught a bus to D.C.

Agatha was horrified when she met me at the station; I could see it in her face.

But she pretended everything was all right, and I moved into their spare room and never told Agatha where I went when I left the apartment. She didn't ask.

We both waited for William to come home, each in our way.

He came back. And wasn't happy that I was there. But he was always polite, coldly polite, around me. Then one night, I overheard them arguing through the walls. About me. Agatha told him to be quiet or he would wake the baby and he said he didn't give a shit who he woke. Then I heard him hit her. She fell to the floor. I heard it. I felt the thud through the thin wall. He left.

I wanted to call 911 but Agatha wouldn't let me. It would hurt his career if there were a police report. So we put an ice pack on her eye and pretended it didn't happen. He came home and apologized, and they both cried, then made loud love. I heard it through the thin wall, putting my hand on my cheek to remember that long-ago kiss so close to my lips. In the morning I taught her how to cover the bruise with makeup, something I learned in those department stores in New York.

I left the apartment later that morning. Back to the streets. I found my man, and he said I could have all the shit I wanted, but I was going to have to earn my keep. So I started hooking.

I would phone Agatha now and then, just to hear how she was doing. William redeployed, to Afghanistan this time. She wanted me to come back, but I said no.

I got busted. Six months in county jail. I barely made it through. Cold turkey. And nobody cared. But my man was waiting for me when I came out. Back on the streets, now on the needle. *Life is good.*

Agatha had to go to the hospital for an operation. The doc said she could never have a baby again, and she said she was afraid to tell William. I told her that he was a tough guy, he could live with it.

He beat her again. Bad this time. She phoned, asked me to come to the hospital. I told her I would hurt him if he ever did this to her again. Nobody had the right to do this to my older sister. Not even William. But she calmed me down. We reported it as an accident at home. The doctor didn't believe us but who gave a shit. We didn't want it to show up on William's record.

I couldn't stay in D.C. after that. I knew he would beat her again. These guys always do. But I would hurt him the next time. I knew I would. I was a skank and a hooker, but I was now a mean-edged skank and hooker who didn't take shit from anyone.

My first night back in New York and I was back in the slammer. No pimp, no money, no protection, no score. I was easy game for the undercover vice cop who cheated by flashing a wad of bills at me. Again cold turkey in a putrid, 9 x 12 cell surrounded by assholes that didn't care.

Agatha told me over the jailhouse phone that they were being transferred to New York, to some military base in Brooklyn, Fort Hamilton. Like, wow, I'm happy for them.

My cellmates introduced me to JayCee when I got out. Back in business. But smarter now, with better protection, and a steady supply of whatever shit I needed, turning tricks on the street, earning my keep, so to speak.

Midnight. On the East Side. William rolls down the street in a nice car. He coasts up to me, the window already down, looks right at me and starts talking, asking me, "How you doing, girl? Looking good. Nice boots," not recognizing me. My heart sank. I knew him instantly. Same beautiful guy. But harder. Lines around his eyes. Gaunt. A smile with no warmth. I got in.

We went down the block, not talking. Parked in the alley behind the 42nd Street terminal. I started with my hand, warming him up. Then I leaned over and kissed him on the lips. A real no-no. Every john knows it's a no-no. They don't expect it. But William took it with enthusiasm, pushing his tongue into my mouth. Pulling me closer, hands all over me. It felt . . . good.

The words came out before I could stop them, "Oh, William."

He stopped with the hands, backed off, looking at me. "Y-you know me?"

"How's Agatha?"

"Oh, shit, it's you."

"Yeah, asshole, it's—" I did not see the punch coming. I'd been hit a lot of times, but this was the hardest slam I ever met. No pain. Just a kaleidoscope of colors, flashes of light, and a desperation to hold onto consciousness. I was bunched against the door, being pounded. I found my straight razor and swung it hard. Any other man would be wearing an ugly scar across his cheek for the rest of his life, but William caught my wrist and took it away from me like he was playing with a two-year-old. Go Army.

I thought he was going to use it to cut me. But he leaned over to open the door to boot me out. Into the filthy, littered street. Then he drove off. He yelled something, but I was too incoherent to understand. Or to care. I lay, curled up on the street, until a squad car drifted past. The pigs got out, laughing. "*Wooweee*, some john got his money's worth tonight."

I used my one call to ask Agatha for help. It hurt to the bottom of my soul to make that call, but I had no one else to reach out to. Their nanny said Agatha wasn't there; she was just taken to the hospital. The girl didn't want to talk about it but finally confessed, sobbing, that William came home in a rage and beat Agatha nearly to death. She, the nanny, was quitting as soon as she could. Just as soon as she could.

It was a week before I could get Agatha back on the phone. Great conversation: I was in the joint on the house phone and she was using the phone next to her hospital bed.

"You gotta leave him, Agatha. You gotta. Divorce the bastard and walk away."

"I can't."

Silence. Both sides.

"I—I still love him."

More silence.

"It's my fault. I-I make him do it. He says I make him do it. M-maybe I do. I don't know. Maybe I do. H-he's been different since he returned from Afghanistan. But we're working on it. W-we are. The Army—"

I hung up. There was nothing more to say. I went to sleep that night in my cell, staring at the ceiling, remembering the kisses. The first kiss, on the cheek, close to my lips. Then the kisses in the car, his hands on me. My hand . . . on him.

We'd never be free of him if I didn't do something. There had to be an end to all of this. I realized what I had to do. We had to be away from him.

The plan: I would keep close contact with Agatha, pretending to be concerned about her recovery. Know where they were going, what they were doing. Biding my time until the opportunity came.

Agatha bought it, pleased that I was taking such an interest in them. She wanted me to visit, to see her and little Billy, when William was away on business. But I pushed that away. She wouldn't want to see me as I was: a street hooker, a skank, a smackhead living from needle to needle. And William definitely would not want to see me again. Agatha's voice on the phone was enough. She saw me as she used to remember me. That was enough.

The opportunity came. William was scheduled to come back to New York on the train. Agatha was to meet him at Penn Station at 4 p.m. on Friday. They were going to stay the weekend in the city. How sweet.

I 'jacked the car on the upper east side, in front of a brownstone. The idiot driver left his motor running while he delivered a pizza. I grabbed the *PIZZA PIZZA* delivery sign off the roof, threw it on the passenger seat, and took off. An old, battered, blue Taurus. Cops wouldn't blink an eye unless I screwed up with a traffic violation.

I parked on the side street, on the corner, so I could see the front of the hotel. They'd be coming out for dinner. Just a matter of waiting, and luck. I put the pizza sign back on top, hoping nobody would bother me for waiting too long in one spot.

Seven thirty p.m. They came out. They'd been arguing again. You could see it from their body language. They separated when they crossed the street, she running away from him. I couldn't believe my luck. Enough space between them for a clean hit.

I gunned the Taurus with a screech of tires. They both stopped in their tracks to see what was going on.

The body actually spun off my hood in a cartwheel, then scudded along the street like a rag doll, no bones, no stiff joints, *flop, flop, flop*. It stopped. I deliberately ran over it just to be sure. *Bump, bump.*

I watched in the rear view mirror as I sped off. William kneeling over Agatha's dead body, looking at the car. But we're both free of him now. Forever. I can no longer feel that soft kiss on my cheek, so close to my lips.

TruckStop Heist

HIS BRASSIERE SLIPPED and the thick wad of paper towels spilled out to bunch at the waist of his blouse, so now he looked like a woman with one tit and one very large love handle. This was not the look he wanted. Worse, thanks to the high-heeled pumps, he wobbled across the parking lot like a drunk. The wig itched, too, never mind the pantyhose riding up his butt crack or the panties squeezing his manhood.

"No one said you had to wear the whole goddamned get-up," Jenkins snapped. "You coulda wore your own underwear for godsakes."

"You said to dress up like a woman. You never—"

You fucking forgot to shave, too."

"I put on foundation."

"And your whiskers are poking through. Looks like dead grass in a snowfield. You are definitely one ugly broad."

Stephen sighed. The whole point, as Jenkins had explained to him a hundred times, was to look like a broad. Ugly or not, who cared? Jenkins said it would outwit the surveillance cameras. Two broads robbing the joint. Nobody'd guess it was a couple of guys. They'd change back into their own clothes when they got back in their car on the way out of there.

"Where's your gun?"

"In my shoulder bag."

They stopped at the door of the TruckStop.

"Can you get it out?"

"Now?"

"Just make sure it's handy."

Stephen snapped open the shoulder bag. The idea of the big shoulder bag was to hold the cash, once they got it in hand. The gun was buried down there somewhere. Everything had settled to the bottom. "Goddamnit, I know it's in here."

"Jeez, you sound like my freaking wife. Don't yank it out now. Wait 'til we get to the cash register. But when we get into the store, go to the bathroom and straighten yourself out so you look presentable for godsakes. We want them to think we're real women. Like Selma and Louise, you know?"

"Selma and who? What are you talk—"

"Never mind. I'll wander around, look like I'm shopping, until you come out, and then we make our move. Got it?"

Stephen nodded. "Yeah. Yeah, I got it." He hated it when Jenkins bossed him around. Jenkins held the door open, smiling encouragement, obviously wanting to build up Stephen's courage. "Now, go," he said.

The toilets were in the back. He took a side aisle, between the bread and bottle coolers, avoiding the cash register.

A man was coming out of the toilet as he went in. Stephen held the door for him. The man glanced over and started to say, "Sorry, that's the men's . . .," then did a double take and blurted, "Oh, oh, my God, you're one of those."

"One of those? Whattaya mean, one of those?"

"I mean . . . never mind . . . use any toilet you want, okay? It's none of my business."

Stephen stared at the guy as he walked away. What the hell was he on about?

Thank God, the bathroom was empty. He opened his blouse to scoop up the loose paper towels, pushing them back into the brassiere cup, but then decided he'd best tighten up the brassiere so the paper wouldn't fall out again. He pulled the blouse off to tighten the strap behind him, then hoisted the blouse back on. While he was at it, he might just as well dump the panties. They were killing him. He couldn't concentrate with all that squeezing. So he lifted his skirt to roll down his pantyhose as he stepped out of the stupid high-heeled shoes, then peeled off the panties with a sigh of relief. He put the panties in the trash bin and started to wrestle the pantyhose back up, just as two men walked into the bathroom.

Both were large, doughy-looking guys, wearing work overalls. Stitching on the chest pockets said "Hudson HVAC."

They stopped dead in their tracks. "Holy shit," one of them said.

"You gotta problem?" Stephen asked, dropping his skirt back into place.

"I ain't ever seen a real pervert before."

"You ain't seeing one now."

The younger man gestured with his hands, taking in Stephen's entire presentation. "Then what are we looking at?"

"I'm leaving, okay?"

"You too fucking homely to use the women's room?"

Stephen sighed. No matter what he said, he knew this was going to turn ugly. He reached into the shoulder bag for the gun, fumbled around for a moment, but found it. He wrenched it out with a flourish and said, "I've had enough of this shit. Give me your clothes."

"What?"

"You guys are about my size, maybe a little bigger. Give me your clothes. They'll fit. Shoes, too. Between the two of you, I should be able to get out of here."

"You gonna shoot us for our clothes?"

"Maybe I'll just jam this gun up your ass."

The younger one smiled, apparently not taking him seriously yet. "That might be fun."

"Who's the pervert now?" Stephen said, waving the gun back and forth between the two of them. "I may not shoot you in the head, but I sure as hell can shoot you in the foot. That'll hurt."

The older man looked down at his shoes, shocked. "You can't do that. I just bought them. They cost me a fortune. Steel-toed, you know?"

"You don't get them off in five seconds, I'm gonna turn them into steel-toed sandals."

The older man stepped behind his younger colleague as if to shield himself. He was now definitely taking Stephen seriously.

Stephen motioned for them to move over to the wash basin, telling them to take off their clothes while he walked over to lock the toilet door. "We don't need more company," he said.

Both men stood at the wash basin, not moving.

"I told you to take your clothes off," Stephen repeated.

"C—can we use the stalls?"

"Take them off out here, where I can see you."

"C—can we keep our billfolds?"

"We're robbing the goddamned store. Might as well start with you guys. Give me your billfolds, watches, and any money you got in your pockets."

Somebody rattled the doorknob, then pounded on the door.

"Piss off," Stephen shouted. "We're busy in here."

"Stephen, what are you doing in there?"

It was Jenkins.

"I'm busy for the moment. I'll be right out."

"What are you—"

"Piss off for the moment, okay?"

Silence. Then he heard the clump of high heels as Jenkins walked away.

He started to take off his own clothes. It wasn't easy doing it with one hand, but he didn't dare put the gun down on the wash counter. The blouse and skirt were easy, but the pantyhose were troublesome, as usual, so he tore them off, finally peeling them off his feet. But he couldn't reach the back of the brassiere with just one hand, so he decided to leave it on. He doubted if either one of these guys wanted it. He left the wig on too. That would confuse people.

The younger guy was taller, so he took his overalls, socks, and boots. It was easy to slip into the loose work clothes and boots with just the one hand, while he waved the gun around the air.

"Y—you want our underwear, too?"

Stephen hesitated, then said, "Yeah."

The older, shorter guy, dared to say, "That's disgusting."

Stephen did not respond. He didn't want to wear the underwear. He just wanted for the two men to be completely naked. They would hesitate before running out the door in their birthday suits. He stuffed their underwear into his shoulder bag, along with their billfolds, watches, loose change, and the extra pair of boots. He rolled the other man's overall under his arm. He would dump it outside in the store somewhere.

"We're done here, guys," he said. "Have a nice day." He kicked his woman's clothes across the floor. "You can share these, or fight over them."

He unlocked the door and peeked out. Another man was waiting patiently. He stepped out, closing the door carefully behind him. "I wouldn't go in there, if I were you," Stephen said. "It's a mess."

Jenkins was standing in the back of the store, looking at the rack of paperback books and magazines. He spun around angrily. "Where the hell have you be—" Then he stopped short. "What the hell?"

"I can explain later. Are we gonna do this or not?"

"Jesus, you went from one very ugly looking broad to one very weird looking handy-man."

"Let's just get this over with," Stephen said. And they did. The woman at the cash register was quite intimidated by the guns, and therefore very cooperative, but also somewhat wide-eyed at the strangest couple she had ever seen. They stuffed the cash into their large shoulder bags and walked out, waving at the surveillance cameras as they went. But the ugly woman in work overalls, with a day-old growth of beard, leaned over to say to the young cashier, "You got two nude perverts in the men's room fighting over women's clothes. The cops are really gonna enjoy your call."

Killers

SHE FELT CONSPICUOUS sitting in the food court at the Mega Mall waiting for a killer. What was she supposed to do? Watch for some mean-looking son-of-a-bitch with a gun in his hand and then stand up to wave and shout, "*Yoo-hoo*, over here?" Like that would be cool.

But she had the props placed on the table that he had asked for: the novel with the bold headline that said *Kill Alex Cross* and a single red rose. Double backup. Any middle-aged broad might have the same novel on her table or maybe even a single red rose, but what were the chances of someone else having both of them? *Spycraft.* That was what it was. She remembered the words from old John le Carré's books. She hadn't thought about that term in twenty years.

Single men came and went. Some sat down for lunch at adjacent tables. Some looked directly at her but that was not surprising. She was a good-looking woman, for her age. She liked that shit, "for her age." The next man who said that to her was going to get the Cross novel shoved up his ass. And she was going to let it age up there.

The table next to her was empty, *thank goodness,* but a couple was weaving through the chairs and other tables as if they couldn't live without this table. *One hundred tables in the food court and you have to pick this one? It's in the back, close to the wall, nearly in a corner. What are you? Recluses? You don't want anyone to see you slurping Singapore noodles?*

"Mrs. Doris Johnson?"

She looked up, totally confused.

The man and woman pulled out chairs to sit down in front of her.

"I thought . . ."

"That I'd be alone?" the man said.

"Yeah. That you'd be alone."

"It's easier this way," the woman said, "No one ever expects an older couple."

"You . . . are . . . Mister . . . Thornton?" Doris asked.

"That will do nicely," Mr. Thornton replied.

"Yes, that will do nicely," the woman added.

Doris pushed the book and rose at them. "Do you want these?" she asked lamely.

The man pushed the book back. "They were just for show." But the woman reached across to take both the book and the rose, saying, "Why not? I haven't read the book, and it is a shame to waste a perfectly beautiful rose." She brushed the rose against her cheek and smiled at the alleged Mr. Thornton. "I can pretend you bought this for me."

Well, ain't that fucking sweet?

Mr. Thornton ignored the woman. *His wife? His mate? His partner? His cover? His what?* "To business, dear Mrs. Johnson, to business. You want us to kill someone."

Doris blinked, not believing she heard the words. Being spoken. Out loud. She had wanted this, had searched for this, had planned this, had waited for this, but it was surreal to hear the words actually being spoken.

"Yes."

"Who?" the woman asked.

Doris slid the photo across the table to the woman.

"Who is this?" Mr. Thornton asked, not bothering to look at the photo.

"Miss Roberta Jacobs."

"May I ask why?"

"She is my husband's girlfriend."

The woman nodded. "Girlfriend or mistress?"

Doris went blank, not understanding the nuances of the question.

"A girlfriend is someone that your husband bangs from time to time or even quite often. A mistress is someone your husband is keeping in an apartment, giving her a car, you know, keeping her."

"What's the difference? I mean, to you? Why would you care, if she was one or the other?"

"The price to you, my dear," Mr. Thornton said. "One of the categories is more expensive than the other."

"Wh-which is cheaper?" Doris asked. *I can't believe that I just said that!*

"Girlfriend."

"She's his girlfriend."

"We can verify, you know," the woman said. "A mistress costs more in upkeep. Therefore you should probably pay more, to relieve your husband of that upkeep."

"Girlfriend," Doris repeated.

The woman flipped the photo over to see the address, phone number, and e-mail address on the back. "Hers, I presume?"

Doris nodded dumbly.

"When?" the man asked.

The woman smiled at Doris but spoke to the man, "ASAP, darling, ASAP. Mrs. Johnson has made the decision and it is up to us to carry it out."

Mr. Thornton smiled at his lovely wife/mate/partner/cover. "Then we do need to discuss price with Mrs. Johnson, don't we?"

◊◊◊

Roberta Jacobs watched Roger through the window as he walked to his car. She was already feeling lonely. It was seven p.m. on Friday and she would not see him again until next week. He always spent the weekend with his family. *With Doris.* He said he was going to leave Doris. He promised. *But was he going to, really?* In the meantime, he had no way, no excuse, no alibi to get away from Doris on the weekends. Nor on the holidays. Nor on his vacations. He waved at the window just before he climbed into his car. She waved back at him. *You son-of-a-bitch!*

The phone rang.

An older male voice said, "We need to talk."

"Who is this?"

"It is about life or death."

Roberta's first reaction was to hang up, but the voice said, "*Your* life or death."

"What are you . . .?"

"We need to meet."

◊◊◊

A park bench. In November. There were a few joggers going past, some dog walkers, but no one else. It was cold and gray, and no one was out enjoying the park. She pulled her cloth coat tighter around her. This was creepy. *Life or death*, the man had said. *Your life or death.*

A woman sat down beside her. *Where had she come from?* Roberta hadn't even seen or heard her walk up.

"I'm sorry," Roberta said, "But I am waiting for someo—"

"Roberta Jacobs?" the woman asked.

Roberta stared at her without speaking.

"You're waiting for me."

"Bu-But, I spoke to a man . . . on . . . the phone."

"Don't worry about him. You're waiting for me."

"What do you want? The man said life or death?"

"Someone wants to kill you."

"To kill me?"

"Doris Johnson."

"Oh, shit."

"So you know why."

"Oh, shit."

"How is Roger?"

"Oh, Shit."

"Is he worth it?"

Roberta fell silent.

"How much is he worth to you?"

"What?"

"How much is he worth to you?"

"I don't understand."

"Doris Johnson has paid us fifteen thousand dollars. To kill you."

"Us?"

"Doris Johnson has paid us fifteen thousand dollars, to kill *you*," the woman repeated. "Would you like to make a counter offer?"

Roberta didn't dare look at the woman. She focused on a tree, black against the sky, barren of leaves, on the far side of the park.

"Don't think of calling the police," the woman said in a sweet voice. "They have no trace of us. We will just disappear. And poor Doris hasn't a clue how to get back in touch with us. You will just look silly accusing her of something that never happened. But we will be back, sometime in the future, to finish the job, the contract, so to speak."

"This is unreal."

"Not to us."

"How can you be so callous?"

The woman patted Roberta on the shoulder and stood up to leave. "It's just business, dear. Nothing personal. Your counter offer. One day to think about it."

"How—how will I get in touch with you?"

But the woman was already walking away.

◊◊◊

They sat in the parking lot of the Brooks Brothers outlet. "Who's going to do it?" the man asked.

"I think I should," the woman said.

The man handed her the small .38 Special. "Don't forget your gloves. Best to make it look like a suicide, if you can. One shot on the side of the head. But don't take any chances. Leave the gun in the car. The serial number has been filed off. The cops will never be able to trace it. I bought it from a doper last month, and it probably went through a dozen hands before it got to him."

The woman smiled. "And you will be here waiting for me."

"As always, dear."

They saw their victim walking to the car.

"It's time, dear."

The woman stepped out of their car to move into the blind spot behind the automobile in front of them. The door opened, and the driver threw in a shopping bag and started to crawl in behind the steering wheel.

The woman moved quickly, blocking the driver's door. Roger Johnson turned his head to see what was happening, but he was too late. The woman jammed the barrel of the gun against the side of his head, an inch above his ear, and fired. He slumped sideways into the passenger seat. She wrapped his left hand around the gun, then closed the door and walked away.

The man drove carefully out of the lot, not hurrying, not drawing attention to their car. They would ditch it ten blocks away, then drive away in their own car, just in case surveillance cameras might have caught this car on tape.

"That went well," the man said.

"It did."

"An easy thirty-thousand dollars."

"Was the shot too loud? Did it attract attention?"

"Sounded like another car noise. No big deal."

They rode for a couple of blocks in silence before the woman added, "I am glad the girls got together. He really was the bastard in all of this, wasn't he?"

"Don't get emotional about it, dear. It's just business."

SUICIDE

THE EXPRESSION on his face said, *Piss off, this is none of your business.* He was standing at the top of a short stepladder, facing me. One end of the rope was secured to the overhead garage beam. The other end formed an expert hangman's noose circling his neck. He kicked away the ladder as I stepped through the door.

I lunged forward to wrap both arms around his legs to lift up just as he hit the end of the rope. There was a sharp jerk and a heavy grunt, but I pushed upward with all my strength.

"You okay?" I could tell he was alive. We had a delicate balance, me carrying the brunt of his weight, his neck straining against the taut rope. I couldn't raise my head high enough to see his face. In fact, I was talking into his crotch.

Silence. Then a gasping. "What . . . the fuck . . . do you . . . think you're doing?"

"What the fuck do *you* think I'm doing?"

"Meddling."

"Don't bother to say thanks."

"I hope . . . you're . . . not . . . a pervert."

"I feel you getting a hard on, I'll drop you. That a deal?"

"This . . . is . . . a mistake."

"Hanging yourself, or my stopping you from hanging yourself?"

"Hanging . . . myself."

"Just had a change of mind, huh?"

"How . . . you gonna get me down?"

I hadn't given that any thought. I was too busy holding him up. I looked around, awkwardly. The stepladder was out of reach and there was nothing else within six feet of us.

"You got . . . a knife on you?" His voice now a hoarse whisper.

"I have a Swiss Army knife, but it's at home."

"My hero."

"If I lift you up, can you put your feet on my shoulders? Then you can reach the beam to untie the rope."

"I got a rope . . . cinched tight around my neck . . . and you want me to balance on your shoulders to reach the beam?"

"Okay. I'll lift you up just a little to put some slack in the rope, then you use your thumbs to loosen the knot around your neck. Maybe you can pull the noose up and off?"

"Okay."

I pushed up as I high as I could and he inserted his thumbs inside the noose, but the shift in weight made me lose my balance and lurch backward. He gagged with a loud squawk, his eyes popping out like huge marbles as the noose cinched even tighter.

"Sorry."

"My . . . fucking . . . thumbs . . . are caught . . . under the noose!"

"I guess that eliminates trying to reach the beam?"

"This . . . really . . . really . . . hurts."

"You were going to hang yourself and you didn't think it would hurt?"

"I thought . . . it was going . . . to be . . . a little quicker . . . than this."

"Why not sleeping pills? Or gas yourself in your car?"

"I'm . . . flat broke. Didn't want . . . to waste . . . a hundred bucks . . . on fancy sleeping pills . . . just to kill . . . myself. And . . . my car . . . repo'd . . . last week."

I shifted my arms, trying to avoid a cramp.

"Be . . . careful . . . will ya?"

"I guess you're not Catholic?"

". . . the fuck . . . has that . . . got to do . . . with anything?"

"Catholics think you go to hell when you commit suicide."

"I'm about . . . to die here . . . and you're . . . worrying . . . about me . . . going to hell?"

"Sorry I mentioned it."

"You . . . Catholic?"

"No."

"Then . . . why the hell . . . bring it up?"

"Just making conversation 'til we figure out what to do. Why you doing it in Chuck's garage, anyway?"

"Chuck . . . away . . . for the weekend. . . . Had nowhere else . . . to go. Why . . . you here?"

"Chuck said I could use his hedge trimmer. Just come over and get it out of the garage while he's away."

"You . . . friend of . . . Chuck's . . . too? Surprised . . . we haven't . . . met."

"Just lucky up to now, I guess."

"What the . . . hell . . . does that . . . mean?"

"Your friend's away and you hang yourself in his garage? He comes home and finds you hanging. He's in shock but has to get you down, call the police, explain who you are, then clean up the mess. Who the hell wants to be your friend?"

"Schmuck . . . deserves this. Got me . . . into this."

A ring tone went off over my head. "You gotta cell phone?"

"Shirt . . . pocket."

"Who's ever calling can help us out for chrissakes!"

"You . . . gonna reach . . . it? My thumbs' . . . trapped upside . . . my neck!"

Pure sarcasm. He knew damn well that I couldn't reach it. The ringing stopped.

"Probably . . . the bitch . . . anyway."

"That's what this is all about?"

"I am . . . flat ass . . . broke. Lost my job. . . . Bitch says . . . we ain't . . . got a . . . future . . . together. No place . . . to go . . . except . . . end of this rope."

"She sounds a bit shallow."

"You . . . a marriage . . . counselor?"

"If you were in love, you could work it out."

"Thank you . . . Dr. Phil. . . . She doesn't . . . work. . . . Just a housewife. . . . Her old man . . . barely . . . has a pot . . . to piss in. . . . Wouldn't get . . . a dime . . . if she divorced him."

"She's married?"

"Neighbor. . . . Chuck . . . introduced us. . . . Thought we . . . would be . . . a real match. . . . So he deserves to . . . find me here . . . stretched out . . . in his garage. . . . Ruin his day."

"Does she know you're this depressed?"

"Saundra . . . only worries . . . about herself."

"Saundra?"

"Yeah . . . Saundra. . . . Only worries about . . . her-self. . . . No money . . . no honey. . . . And I ain't got . . . no money."

I shrugged my shoulders, lifting his legs a few more inches, "I don't think we're going to make it."

"We . . . not going . . . to make it? What . . . does . . . that mean?"

"I can't see any way out of this and I am getting tired of holding you up."

"You . . . going . . . to drop me . . . just like that?"

"Yeah."

So I dropped him. He bounced and gurgled and danced in the air and turned blue and purple, his eyes bugging out again, then fell silent.

I spent a few minutes looking for Chuck's hedge trimmer, then giggled on the way out thinking about Chuck finding his buddy hanging in the garage. How was he going to explain about the thumbs caught up under the noose?

But I was anxious to get home. I couldn't wait to tell my wife, Saundra, that I met her boyfriend.

Totally Off the Rails

THEY

I AM MAD. Irrevocably insane. Everyone says so. Because I see strange things in the cornfield behind our house in the late evening.

They are not ghosts. But their bodies are pale, transparent, shimmering, never firm. Their movements blend between a flickering dance and an erratic darting around, like water bugs on a stagnant pond. And I hear their voices. Nothing verbal. More like musical tones. High pitches mixed with low notes. Like chimes. The sounds do not sound menacing, but they do cause unease, a foreboding.

My husband, Earl, laughed at me in the beginning. He would watch me standing out on the patio, staring at the cornfield as the sun went down, waiting for them, and he would mock me. "Are you seeing your cornfield people again, Sweetie?" I would point at them, when they finally came, but he could never see them. I would motion for him to be quiet, but he could never hear them, either. But I could see them, and I could hear them, and there were more and more of them every week.

Earl finally got angry. He put on his hunting clothes and hiking boots, pulled out his shotgun and loaded it, took his good flashlight, the kind the police use. "If there is something out there, by God, I'll find them and chase them away. Are you gonna come along or not?"

I backed away. No way was I going out there, and I didn't want him to go. But he slammed the back door and left.

He came back empty handed and even angrier. "There is nothing out there," he said. "Nothing. So stop your damn nonsense now."

But more of them came. A few more each evening. I saw them weaving in and out of the rows of corn and through the far trees, singing to one another, whistling to get one another's attention, as if they were exploring a new world around them. I dared not stop watching. I couldn't take the time to cook supper for Earl anymore, and I no longer had the time to come inside to watch television. Earl had to come out to steer me back into the house to go to bed. Some nights I'd slip back out to watch, but he always caught me and got really upset.

He took me into the city to see the doctor. I am physically fine, the doc said. Blood pressure a little high, but nothing to be worried about yet. A small pill of Diovan every day should take care of that. I am in great shape for a woman my age, yes, indeed, he said. But he added two more prescriptions for Earl to take to the drugstore. Xanax and Prozac. If one didn't work, we could try the other.

The first one made me drowsy for most of the day. Not getting anything done. Didn't really care, either. A nuclear bomb coming down our chimney wasn't going to bother me much. But they were still out there. Coming closer. I could tell.

We moved on to the second prescription. But we must have overdone the dose because I was now lost in my own head. Dreams. Memories. Long periods of nothing. Earl had to feed me and take me back to my bed.

Then come back to take me to the toilet, if it wasn't already too late. In the afternoons, I'd lie on the sofa and stare at the ceiling while he cleaned the sheets and did the laundry.

But I could still hear them. Late at night. Their songs penetrated the gray fog of the pills. They were coming closer. Now almost to the edge of the back yard. Fully awake for the first time in days, I slipped out of bed, trying not to wake Earl, to stand on the patio in my nightgown. They were looking at me now, pointing. Talking at me. I could tell. It was a warm summer evening, but I felt a chill and needed to hug my arms around my body to keep warm.

Earl came busting out of the sliding glass doors, mad as hell, saying I am goddamn crazy standing out there in the middle of the night in my bare feet and half nude. He hit me. For the first time in our married life, he hit me. In the morning I had a huge black eye, but I couldn't remember where it came from. But Earl was crying and hugging me and saying he was sorry and he would never do it again and I gotta forgive him. I didn't know what he was talking about. Didn't care, either.

We went into the city to see another doctor. But this one didn't give me any pills. At least not then. Just talked to me. And talked and talked and talked. Asked me stupid questions about my family and about my father and about how I felt about Earl and if we were still having sex and did I feel like going somewhere for a rest?

I told him I didn't want to go nowhere. I didn't need to rest. I needed to stay home. To watch them. They were getting closer.

He and Earl had a long talk afterward. More pills. No big surprise in that. But then a woman came into the house to watch after me while Earl was off at work. I didn't remember her name. But she was pleasant enough.

Fed me well. Made sure I made it to the toilet. Let me sleep. Earl came home after work to take over. Gave me a lot more pills at bedtime.

But they didn't work. I could still hear them out there. But I couldn't get up to see them now, as Earl had me strapped down on a cot in the spare bedroom. I couldn't move my wrists or ankles. But they were talking to me, now just outside the windows.

Earl had to go on a trip for work, so the woman came to stay day and night. It was going to work out. She put together a schedule for me, for when to eat and when to pee and when to do the other things I needed to do. She dressed me and fit on my shoes for me. It was nice, I thought.

One night she saw me listening and trying to look out the window. Asked what I was hearing. I told her. She nodded and smiled to herself. Then untied me to walk me out to the back patio.

They were there. Excited at seeing someone new. But she didn't see them. Or hear them, just like Earl. I took her hand and pulled her past the patio into the yard so she could be closer to them. Surrounded by them. But she put her hands on her hips and stared around the yard and out into the cornfields and into the trees and said she didn't see or hear a thing. That made me so mad I picked up the rake Earl had left in the yard and hit her with it. Again and again. Damn her. Damn her. Damn her. Broke the handle but I kept hitting her with the rake head.

They took her away. That surprised me. They took her by the arms and legs and pulled her into the forest.

Earl came home two days later and asked me why the woman wasn't there. He was really angry. The house was disheveled and my clothes were soiled and the toilets were backed up. I told him. I told him they took her.

Out into the trees. Which made Earl even angrier. He hit me again. Said I was lying. Said I drove the woman away. Said I was a crazy bitch and he couldn't take it anymore. I said she was out there in the trees. With them.

He looked at me funny. Then went out the back door, telling me to stay there, he'd be right back.

I watched him go and I knew what I needed to do.

Took him a long time but he came storming back, even angrier than before. I was waiting for him at the back door. I blasted him with the shotgun. The first barrel stopped him—straight up. The second barrel blew him past the patio table, right out into the yard.

I sat down on the patio chair to wait. They came in the evening, really excited to snatch another body. They dragged Earl away, singing and whistling just as I thought they would.

So now I'm waiting here at the house with the shotgun to see if anyone else will show up. They'd like that.

Choices

"YOU ARE AWARE that you are dead?"

The man talking to me was wearing immaculate white hospital scrubs. Middle-aged. Almost handsome, in an effete way. Good head of brown hair. The only thing lacking was a stethoscope around the neck. But if he was a doctor (or a nurse), it was obvious no one had thrown up or bled out on him today.

"Yes, I kinda thought something like that was going on," I replied. I pointed at the casket sitting on the dais in the front of the viewing room. "That's me in the coffin, right?"

We were sitting at the back of the room. A handful of people were seated in chairs in front of us, either praying or meditating or just staring at the wall as a way of passing a long afternoon. I couldn't tell which. Others walked up to the coffin, running their hands across the surface and nodding before they walked away. I knew most of them. A couple I didn't. I assumed they came in for the cookies and coffee being served in the hallway and thought it was polite to do a pass-by over the coffin. No one seemed to notice us or hear us talking.

"Am I a ghost?"

"No. You are in transition."

"In transition? I'm not a ghost . . . but maybe a spirit?"

"That's one way to look at it. I am happy to see that you are taking this so well."

"Do I have a choice?"

"We'll talk about that in a moment."

"Why is the casket closed?"

"You were mangled."

"Mangled?"

"You were hit by a UPS truck going full speed. Your body and face were completely rearranged, so to speak. You were hard to identify after the truck finished with you. Kinda like road kill wearing clothes. Thank God, you had ID on you. Most squirrels do not have billfolds with them, even if they happen to wear pants."

"I don't remember any of that."

"You were on your cell phone."

"Oh—"

"Texting."

"Oh—"

"In the middle of the crosswalk. The UPS truck had a green light. You were jaywalking. Or should I say jay-standing?"

"That's good. I mean, not that I am dead, but at least the driver won't get into trouble because I was standing there, in the middle of the crosswalk."

"Very noble of you."

"I try."

"We need to talk about your choices."

We heard sobbing. My wife came into the room. Her sister and her pinch-faced cousin were holding her up. I was touched. The pinch-faced cousin wouldn't even come to the house if I were home. I almost reached into my pocket to find my cell phone to text my wife not to take it so hard, but then I remembered I was dead and my cell phone was probably as mangled as I was. I glanced down at myself and was pleased that I was still in the same clothes I wore to work. And they were still neat and pressed. Good trick, considering that I was mangled. I wondered how they did that.

"Choices," the man repeated, calling me back into the conversation.

"Ah, good point. I always wondered about that. When we come back at the redemption or resurrection or whatever you call that, at the end of the world, do we get to choose what age we come back as? I mean, is it necessarily the age we died, or do we get to come back younger? Like middle-aged or even younger, you know what I mean? I wouldn't want to come back as a kid, but a little younger than I am now would be nice. Do we get to choose that?"

"That's not the choices we are talking about."

I crossed my legs, tugging up my pant legs to protect the crease like I usually did. "But this is a real concern," I said. "I've thought about this quite a lot, ever since cataclysm class, when I was real young."

"Catechism. Catechism class. Not cataclysm class, although in your case . . ."

"What? Oh, you know what I mean."

"That's not what we are talking about."

I shut up. He seemed to be agitated as if he had somewhere else he needed to be, but, as I was apparently dead, I wasn't in a rush to go anywhere. At least not somewhere else. I was enjoying watching my funeral. More people than I expected. But I was always good about going to other people's funerals.

"You were killed by an unanticipated accident."

I turned my head to look at my companion. Who was this guy, anyway? He wasn't too smart. I felt it was necessary to correct him. "All accidents are unanticipated. That's why they call them accidents."

The man sighed, ignoring my sarcasm. "That gives you a choice."

"Again with the choices."

"Would you please listen to me?"

"Don't get all pissy on me. I am the one who is dead here, you know, although I don't know what you are. Or who you are."

"Never mind that. Because of the unanticipated accident, for which we apologize, you can either go back to living or take the next step."

I measured his words carefully. "Go back to living or take the next step?"

"Precisely."

"I don't quite understand those choices."

He sighed again as if he found this conversation to be very trying. "If you want to go back to living, we will insert you back just at the moment before you stepped into the street. The whole scene, so to speak, will be reset."

"Will I . . . will I remember this . . . this conversation?"

"No."

"How long will I live if I go back?"

"I can't tell you that."

I sat up straight in my chair. That proposal was a bit frightening. "So, if I go back, I might . . . step in front of the UPS truck again?"

"Could happen."

"Will we then be having this conversation over again? A repeat of all this?"

The man shook his head. "No. Our mistake will have been corrected. If the truck hits you again, it will now be an anticipated accident, and you will proceed directly to the next step."

"That's a bit unfair. If it's the same accident I should be given a second chance."

"This is your second chance," the man said. "We made the mistake. We are now giving you a chance to correct it. You must understand that this offer is very rare. Very rare. It was discussed at the highest levels. The very highest levels. You should realize this . . . and appreciate it."

"You screwed up, and I should appreciate it?"

The man fell silent. My wife, her sister, and her pinch-faced cousin had left the room. I thought they would stay longer. But knowing them, they probably wanted to go shopping.

"How long will I live if I make it across the street, without being hit by the truck?"

"I can't tell you that. I just told you, I can't tell you that."

I wondered if I could go to the hallway to get a cookie and some coffee. This conversation was starting to depress me. "So, I could make it across the street and then have a heart attack, or something could fall on me out of the sky, and I only gained a few more minutes? What kind of deal is that?"

"The only one I can offer you."

I stood up to stretch my legs. This being dead was getting old. "And if I don't go back to living?"

"We move on to the next step."

"Which is?"

"I can't tell you that."

"Excuse me?"

The man shifted uncomfortably in his chair. "If you do not go back, you will then be immediately processed like everyone else. I cannot tell you what the next step will be because that will influence your choice. It's like the games you people used to play on television. Choose door one or door two, but we can't tell you what is behind either. Your life, your death, your choice."

I sat back down. This was now making me angry. I appreciated they were giving me a choice. From the very highest levels. They were giving me choices. But not good choices. "May I ask your advice?"

"No."

"What's your name? You can at least tell me that. I might want to make a report later. Answer a survey or something, you know? I might put in a good word for you. Or not."

"My name is immaterial to you. Please make your choice."

I surveyed the viewing room. The crowd was diminishing. With a little effort, if I went back, I could try to make a few more friends. I could really make an effort at being social, maybe even a better person. I bet I could influence a better choice for "the next step" if I tried harder.

"I'm going back."

"That is your choice?"

"It is my—"

I was on Hayes and Fourth Street, having a strange moment. I had a fleeting memory of a conversation that seemed surrealistic, like I was talking to a guy in white scrubs as if we were at a hospital or something. But it disappeared like a wisp of smoke. *A senior moment?* I was obviously walking home. I had a green light, but I had to hurry as the light was about to change. My phone beeped just as I stepped into the street. I stopped to see who was texting me.

Pigeon Flying Corps

"THERE MUST BE MORE to life than just eating and pooping," I said, a bit depressed.

Herman did not respond. I heard rustling at the other end of the tree branch. I glanced over. He was staring at a parked car directly below us. He had a smile on his face, or at least as much of a smile as a pigeon can smile. He finally noticed me and said, "You hungry?"

"Did you hear a word I just said?"

"Did you see what I just did?"

"Let me guess. You just pooped on the car."

"BMW. Splat dead center on the windshield. Best shot of the week."

This is it? Junk food and precision bombing? Are these the highest personal goals a pigeon could look forward to?

"Let's celebrate, Ozzie. They had a baseball game at the stadium last night. Late innings, really late. Lights were on all night, which means at least half of the people were drunk and spilling peanuts and throwing french fries at each other. Could be a righteous harvest."

"They're using red tailed hawks at the stadium now. Peregrine falcons, too. Using them to keep us away. Vicious big buggers."

Herman groaned. "That's not right, just not right. All that food just lying there and those stupid hawks don't

107

even appreciate it. They'd rather eat mice, for chrissakes. Desperate little mice. They call us scavengers, and we're the ones who won't eat mice."

"Unjust stereotyping," I said, tongue in cheek.

Herman did not catch my sarcasm. "But they don't eat us," he said, puffing out his chest in anger. "Pure harassment, that's all it is. Rip out a few tail feathers, take a head nip, rake us with those vicious, long talons. If I were bigger, I would—"

At that moment I saw a gaggle of Canada geese flying high above us in a tight V-formation, heading no doubt to the small lake in the city park on the other side of town. *Talk about eaters and poopers. Nothing but oversized, foul honkers who forgot how to migrate. They come down from Canada and stay, not making any effort to go farther south, and too lazy to go back home when the weather changes. Who needs 'em?*

But—they just gave me an idea.

Herman didn't notice me gazing at the geese. "The old lady should be out on her stoop by now, throwing out crumbs. Good bread," he said.

"Day-old bread."

"Like somebody is gonna throw us fresh bread?"

"Let's find Swenson. I have an idea."

Herman grunted. "What do we need him for? He's always in a bad mood. He shoulda been a damned crow."

"He'll work with us."

"Work with us? What does that mean?"

"Trust me."

We found Swenson in his usual place, the window ledge at the idle paper cup factory, behind the Sonic drive-through. He made his living off the scraps that the drivers spilled out of their car windows and lunch trays, and the busted trash bags jammed into the waste bins behind the restaurant. A great gig for an old guy.

But neither Swenson or Herman listened to me as I walked back and forth on the window sill, excitedly explaining my idea. Herman was distracted by the goodies lying on the driveway, while Swenson eyed him closely, daring the younger dude to make a swoop on his territory. Herman knew he would pay for it dearly if he did, but the temptation was almost stronger than he could handle. I had to talk fast before the shit hit the fan, metaphorically speaking.

Swenson looked at me skeptically with one eye, the other on Herman. "You want us to learn to fly in formation? Like a bunch of geese? What the hell for?"

"It's only the first step, but it'll be worth it, I promise."

"What's the second step?"

"I'll explain it afterward, if we make it work. Otherwise, we'll just drop it—Herman, are you listening to any of this?"

"That fool just dropped a whole bag of nachos."

"Those are my nachos," Swenson said.

"Not if I beat you to them."

I ruffled my feathers and stepped between them. "Guys, listen to me. I'm promising you something better. And we won't have to fight over it."

"Do I have to work with him?" Swenson said, backing away from Herman in disgust.

"You're on to something good and you want to leave me out of it, huh? Is that it?" Herman said, making a weak attempt to stare down Swenson.

I knew I had them with that. I dived from the ledge, swooping away gracefully to catch the wind, yelling over my shoulder, "Follow me."

But we had a rough start.

I instructed Herman to stay on my right, slightly outside and behind me, with Swenson on my left, also outside and behind me. They were to remain parallel to each other when we flew straight. The trouble came when we veered: If I banked right, Swenson had to speed up to stay with me, which was hard for the old man. If I banked left, Herman pulled even with me, and sometimes shot ahead. A straight dive wasn't bad, as they each managed to hold their positions, but pulling up was ragged, with the three of us all over the place. I never thought it would be this hard to get six wings to flap together. *Freaking geese.*

But we stayed with it, getting better. A few other guys saw us cavorting about in formation and joined us for the fun of it. The younger ones caught on quick. I stacked them in the back of the formation as they could fly faster when we banked away from them, keeping the flight pattern tight. I preened with pride. We were turning into a regular Pigeon Flying Corps.

After an hour we settled on the big maple tree on Linden Avenue, tired but pleased with ourselves. "Now what?" Swenson asked.

Herman sighed. "I'm really hungry."

"Relax, recuperate, take care of yourselves, poop if you gotta, then we go on the attack."

"Attack?" several voices asked in surprise.

"To the stadium. We're taking on the hawks and falcons."

"You're kidding me," Herman said in total shock.

"You're the one who said good food, and plenty of it. A righteous harvest, to quote you, just lying around over there."

"I'm too old for this," Swenson said.

"Not if we hang together. We swoop in, keeping tight formation, protecting each other. No one gets isolated. The hawks and falcons are all loners. So we take them on one at a time."

One of the younger guys flapped a wing to get my attention. "But if we break formation when we finally go down for the food, they'll pick us off one by one."

"Here's the key," I said in my most somber voice, now the voice of a leader. "One of us has to go down first, alone, as bait. They won't pay any attention to the rest of us flying in formation overhead. They'll think we're a gaggle of stupid geese. Then when one of them makes a move on our guy, we dive. We take him apart. Then do it over again, and again, until the stadium is all ours."

The group digested all of this silence. A few hopped back and forth on the tree limb, thinking it through.

"It's fool proof," I said.

"So who is going to be the bait?" Swenson asked.

I looked around. "We need a volunteer."

Dead silence.

"I can't do it. I'm the leader of the formation," I said.

"I can lead the formation," Swenson said.

"With all due respect, you're too old, too slow."

"Where the hell is the respect in that?"

"I can lead the group," Herman said. "I was in it from the beginning."

No one else spoke out, or volunteered. It became readily apparent that if we were going to do this, I was going to be the bait. It was my idea. I was the leader. I would need to lead from the front.

"Can I depend on all of you?" I asked.

"You know damn well you can depend on me," Herman said, almost offended.

I sighed. "Okay. Let's do it, then."

We jumped off toward the stadium. I flew off to the side and slightly below the formation, letting Herman take the point position, watching to see if he could handle it. He did well. He took them through some easy banking, both left and right, testing them, getting them used to his speed, then dove straight down, the group trailing right behind him. It was going to work. I could see it was going to work.

There were no hawks or falcons in the sky over the stadium, but I spotted three of them sitting on the leather gloves of their human handlers. Both the birds and the humans were scanning the skies, watching for intruders. They disregarded our formation, just as I thought they would, not recognizing it for what it was, *a pigeon formation*. But I could feel their eyes on me, the lone stray, off by myself, flying high over their territory.

The food was there, just as Herman had promised, waiting for us. Long, greasy french fries, cheesy nachos, salted peanuts, dropped hot dogs smothered in mustard, and doughy pretzels. The cleaning staff was working through the rows, seat by seat, large black trash bags on their shoulders, sweeping and picking, but they had just started. There was a lot still down there. Enough for all for us. If we were quick.

I could feel that I was about to become a legend in the pigeon world. Maybe in the entire world of feathers. Even non-flying ostriches would talk about me: the Napoleon of pigeons. I would train other formations. Expand our reach. Control the country. I had found my calling, at last.

It was time. I glanced at my guys. They kept tight formation, looking strong and formidable. I nodded at Herman, acknowledging my confidence in him. He nodded back. I dived.

I went for the high bleachers, for safety's sake. Going too low, for the expensive seats behind home plate, would expose me for too long, giving the raptors time to react. *Stay close to the formation,* I told myself. Stay close so they could quickly keep the bad guys off my back.

I saw the human handlers raise their arms, the raptors glaring at me in anger. The handlers spoke to their birds and they were off, up, batting their huge wings furiously to gain height, not taking their eyes off me.

I went for a busted pretzel with soft white dough spilling out of the hard, brown, salty crust. I had to make a quick decision: hit and run and take the whole pretzel with me, or stop and eat? Could I trust the formation to drive off any intruder that came near me?

The nasty big guys were up now, had their height, and were plunging down. On me. *Now, Herman, now.* I looked back in desperation.

The formation tilted over, homing in on the raptors who didn't see them coming.

But it broke apart. Everyone going in their own direction. The temptation was too much. Some went for the high bleachers, others for the lower bleachers, some for the aisles. So much food, so many pigeons, so little time. The formation, the idea of the formation, was over.

I heard the high, frightening screech of a hawk coming straight at me. I desperately scurried under a bleacher seat. The pressure from his beating wings bore down on me. I buried my head under my wing, waiting for the pain. But he veered away with a shriek. There were too many other moving targets in the stadium for him to bother with just me.

I stretched my neck out to tug the pretzel under the seat beside me, then ate it calmly, nibbling at my leisure. I looked up now and then to determine if I could make my break without too much danger, waiting until the raptors were far too busy ripping at the others to take notice of me.

I managed to sneak away in silence, embarrassed by the carnage that I had caused. But the fear, the tension, and the disappointment had my bowels in an uproar. I glanced over at one of the human handlers and decided to chance a precision bombing on my way out.

ON THE SKRANG

IN HIS OWN smug, self-satisfied way, Richard Turnball felt he was truly *one with nature* at this moment. The South China Sea sparkled in the distance, the late morning sun playing across endless variations of aquamarine and turquoise blue. The rolling hills behind the resort sported a thousand shades of green foliage. But in fact Turnball looked like a pale whale sprawled across a pool lounge chair. He stirred only now and then to sip on a fruity purple drink that sported a silly toothpick umbrella and to puff on a stale cigar.

His center of attention was focused on the handful of attractive women splashing in and out of the pool, who modestly hid their female assets in string bikinis and wet thongs. He thought about pulling his T-shirt back on to protect his bleached-white protruding belly from the imposing tropical sun but he was too relaxed to make the effort.

Rachel would be back soon. She had announced over breakfast that they would go into Kuching this afternoon to see the Grand Bazaar, where she would spend hours shopping for woven baskets, multi-colored sarongs, and cheap sandals carved from tire treads. This tedium would be magnified by her manic need to "bargain" with the natives ("They expect it, you know. It's how they do business.") Turnball would keep his silence, but would inwardly sigh, *if you calculate the exchange rate, you're arguing over twenty-five fucking cents. Give the woman the goddamned quarter and let's move on for God's sake.*

After breakfast she had rushed off to tour the Sarawak Cultural Village, a collection of "authentic" huts and houses that represented the ethnic lifestyles of the semi-naked tribes that used to haunt the local jungles. Turnball had begged off, citing "Borneo Belly." This was their first long weekend together, a short hop from super-modern Singapore to the bush of East Malaysia. He had anticipated a long weekend in bed. She apparently saw it as a weekend adventure for Indiannette Jones. He would put up with it, assuming that even jungle explorers came back to bed now and then.

"Rich, honey, get dressed. I've booked us a tour."

He swiveled around, startled. He did not expect her back this soon. "Uh . . . gee . . . Rach, I don't feel that good yet. Why don't you go and I'll wait for you here."

"It's an overnighter, Rich. Up to an Iban longhouse on the Skrang River. We leave in an hour and come back tomorrow afternoon."

"An Iban longhouse?"

"I'll tell you all about it, but you need to go get dressed. Real quick."

Turnball heard the splash behind him of a scantily clad female diving into the pool. "What about the hotel? We booked the room for the whole weekend."

Rach smiled to show that she was way ahead of him. "They're okay with it. They'll hold our luggage until we come back, then put us in a different room. No big deal. They do it all the time."

His first reaction was to whine a bit, but decided to give in. Whatever an Iban longhouse was, it couldn't be too bad if the resort was tied into it.

A small van waited in front of the hotel, *RiverSafaris* stenciled on the side. They were alone, except for the driver and a guide. The driver wore a black T-shirt, jeans, and dark aviator sunglasses. He did not smile when they climbed into the van. The guide wore a safari shirt with matching slacks and an oily smile. He introduced himself as Ali, and the driver as Hamid.

As they shook hands, Turnball discovered Ali had two thumbs on his right hand. Or a thumb with a hanging appendage. He tried not to look down or to show any shock, but it was upsetting. He waited until Ali turned away before wiping his hand on his slacks.

"There're only two of us?" Rachel asked.

Ali bobbed his head in enthusiasm "Yes, yes. It is not peak season, so you are very fortunate to be on your very own."

Once inside, Rachel leaned over the front seat to say, "Hamid, thank you for driving us."

Hamid grunted but did not turn to acknowledge her. "Hamid does not speak English," Ali said, "but he says you are very welcome."

Great fucking start, Turnball thought. He glanced at the brochure on the seat beside him. This would be a two-and-a-half-hour drive (*two-and-a-half hours?*) followed by a one-hour boat ride up the river to where twenty families lived together in a long house made of wood and bamboo, with a thatched roof. *Great fucking finish, too.*

Rachel continued to chat with Ali as they rolled down the highway. Turnball slouched into full boredom. It quickly became apparent that once you have seen one rubber plantation, you've seen them all: unending miles of trees, all the same height, with the same crown of palms, all in straight anal rows, skirted by dirt paths pounded out by the bare feet of the tappers and sappers.

The only alleviation was the rice paddies, all pancake flat between their berms, with rows of palm trees in the far distance.

Rachel and Ali eventually (*thank God!*) ran out of things to talk about. Ali slumped back against the front seat for a nap. Rachel smiled at Turnball. "It's all so beautiful, isn't it?"

Turnball gave an imitation Hamid grunt and pretended to nap, too.

"You're not enjoying this?"

Turnball made an effort to change the subject. He shook his right hand, nodding toward Ali. "Why doesn't he have it removed?" he whispered. "No big deal. An outpatient routine. I could do it myself if I had an axe. Or a machete. A quick whack. Then a little antiseptic and a Band-aid. Done."

"*Shh*, he'll hear you," Rachel said, horrified.

Turnball laughed. "Guy could be a hell of a hitchhiker. A twofer. Double your chances. Might cause an accident with cars piling up behind each other to stop for him."

Rachel turned away without comment.

The rest of the trip passed in somnolent, irritated silence, until Ali directed Hamid to pull over for refreshments and a toilet break at a roadside shantytown that consisted of several crumbling huts with corrugated tin roofs.

The restaurant looked like a pool cabana: four posts supporting a thatched roof over a handful of plastic tables and chairs surrounding a small bar. Signs touted Pepsi and Tiger Beer. The Pepsi turned out to be flat and the beer warm. Suffocating heat and humidity radiated up from the dirt floor. Turnball and his beer sweated together.

Rachel came back from the toilet, her usual cheerful self, to order another Pepsi. Turnball took his turn, only to discover the "toilet" was a porcelain slab with foot-pads parallel to a small hole. He couldn't remember the last time he squatted for anything, and he had never in his life sustained a squat with his pants and underwear around his ankles. It was like shitting in a sauna.

He became really pissed when he discovered the lack of toilet paper. There was only a low faucet, dribbling water. *The longhouse had better be better than this*, he thought as he slammed the toilet door on the way out.

"You okay?" Rachel asked.

"Just swell."

Rachel, Ali, and Hamid were eating a brown glop called *mee goreng*. The smell made Turnball gag. His first thought was to rush back to the toilet to vomit, but the toilet was more repulsive than the *mee goreng*, so he sucked on his warm beer and ignored all entreaties to try the food.

Back on the road, Ali became animated. "We are close now, so you should read these," he said, handing over brochures titled *Precautions Going To and At the Longhouse*. Turnball scanned the table of contents. His eyes locked on the subheadings of *Viper Tourniquets, Python Killings, Meeting with Crocodiles, and Venomous Spiders*.

"You're kidding, right?"

"All nonsense," Ali said. "Liability precautions, you know? Lawyers? They told the tour owners to distribute these as a precaution. It's nothing, really. Mehdi, the guide who will take you upriver, will take good care of you. Never mind."

"You're not going upriver with us?"

"No, no, I'm a city boy. Hamid, too. We don't like this country stuff, going up the river. But we'll be back tomorrow evening to take you back to the resort. You're going to have great fun."

Rachel was avidly reading the brochure from front to back. *At least one of us will know what to do when some venomous viper or blood-sucking spider attacks us*, he thought cynically.

Several long, narrow canoes were beached on the pebbly shore, with a group of men standing around talking and smoking, dressed in T-shirts, jeans, and baseball caps. One of the men pasted on a smile and hurried forward as the van bumped toward the landing. His smile grew wider when Rachel stepped out of the van. "Hello, I'm Mehdi. Welcome. Very nice to be seeing you."

Huge outboard engines were attached to the sterns of the metal canoes. Mehdi shouted to the other men who immediately manhandled one of the boats into the shallow water. Mehdi motioned for Rachel and Turnball to follow, wading up to their knees to the side of the canoe. Rachel stepped lightly over the gunwale to settle onto a seat. Turnball followed awkwardly, nearly tipping the boat, but Mehdi caught him to guide him in, then settled in behind them, the driver behind him.

The remaining men gave an immense shove and the canoe floated to the middle of the river. The man in the back pulled, over and over, on the rope attached to the oversized Mercury outboard.

Ali and Hamid stood beside the van, shouting, "See you. See you." Or at least Ali shouted and waved. Hamid stood with his arms crossed over his chest, staring at them.

Rachel waved back. "See you tomorrow evening."

Turnball gripped both sides of the canoe and stared straight ahead, reassured when he heard the Mercury outboard finally roar to life. The canoe shot forward as the outboard's propellers bit into the deep channel. The breeze was refreshing, and Turnball relaxed for the first time since leaving the resort, although he had to be careful not to shift around too much, causing the boat to roll with his weight.

After a while, even with the breeze, the sun began to bake. He noted the thick shade that covered both banks and yelled back at Mehdi, "Can't we ride in the shade?" Mehdi couldn't hear him over the outboard, but Rachel passed the message along. Mehdi said something and laughed. Rachel grinned and shouted over the noise, "Mehdi says that is no good. Sometimes the snakes fall out of the trees into the boats. He also says you should not drag your hand in the water. There are sometimes bad things in the water."

Turnball said, "Shit," jerking his hand out of the water.

It took forty minutes to arrive at the longhouse landing. Another collection of canoes with oversized outboards was waiting on that beach, with more men sitting around talking and smoking. A handful of naked children splashed in the shallows and waved to them. The driver killed the motor as several men waded out to pull the canoe to the shore. Mehdi was quickly out of the boat, shouting, "Come. Come."

Rachel slipped over the side and into the water. Turnball started but again tipped the boat. Two men grabbed him by the armpits to save him from a face flop into the river. No one laughed, but he suspected they were snickering behind his back.

Mehdi had Rachel by the arm, leading her to the grass beyond the beach. Turnball heard, smelled, and then spotted a pig pen while chickens grubbed in the dirt in front of him. The clearing was dominated by an immense hovel with a corrugated tin roof, built on stilts. "Your time is good," Mehdi said. "We have time to talk,

then some dances, maybe some shopping, and then supper."

Shopping? Dances?

A huge log notched with footholds substituted as a
ladder up to the veranda, which appeared to be an endless front porch the length of two football fields. A crowd
of people, mostly women and children, milled around in
small groups, gossiping, sewing, cooking, and napping
on the porch floor. No one paid any attention to them.

Mehdi led them to a large straw mat, chasing away
a gaggle of children. "Wait here. I will find the Chief to
welcome you. He will be pleased to talk to you."

"I thought they were expecting us," Turnball said.

"But they didn't know exactly when we would get
here," Rachel replied.

They surveyed the veranda: a blend of Main Street
and front porch for twenty or more families that lived in
the rooms opening onto the deck. The only "primitives"
Turnball saw were a few scraggly toothed, bare-chested
old women in sarongs. The younger women wore flow-
ered print, ankle-length dresses that were fashionable in
Kansas in the 1940s.

"Do you see that?" Rachel said, looking up at the rafters.

"What?" Turnball said, looking up for bats or snakes
or spiders or something else equally menacing, but spotted only a signed poster of Miss Iowa 2007. *Now that was
a woman!*

"In the rafters. The bones and little heads."

"Bones and little heads?"

"These people were headhunters not that long ago."

Turnball squinted harder. "Headhunters?"

"Fierce warriors. Manhood and leadership were
equated with the number of heads that a man could collect. They told us all about it at the Cultural Village."

Turnball finally saw the shrunken heads hidden in the upper notches of the ceiling. "Those are real?"

"This is so cool," Rachel said, just as Mehdi came back with the Chief and a second man. Both of them looked a thousand years old, with leathery, wrinkled skin and stiff knees.

Mehdi squatted beside Rachel. "This is the Chief, the *tuai rumah*, and the shaman. They are pleased to meet you. They do not speak English. I will translate."

"We are honored to meet them," Rachel said.

"Shaman?" Turnball said. "Like medicine man?"

Mehdi nodded. "More or less."

"Do you do voodoo tricks? Or fly around like Harry Potter?" Turnball asked, waving his hands in the air as if conjuring up a magic spell and adding, "*Woooooo!*"

"Richard!"

"I understand," Mehdi said. "A joke." He spoke to the two men. They laughed politely.

"Is there anything else you would like to ask them?"

The only other thing Turnball could think of was *why the freaking hell do you live here?* But Rachel jumped in with a slew of questions about the longhouse, the living arrangements, and the school for the children, causing an endless back-and-forth in two languages that would have put a dedicated missionary to sleep.

Turnball gazed around, noting television sets flickering in some of the rooms and heard Lady Gaga on someone's cassette player. Most of the kids wore shorts and T-shirts, but all were barefooted. The Chief and shaman wore short-sleeved plaid shirts and jeans. *All they're missing are plastic pocket protectors,* Turnball thought.

Flies buzzed everywhere, causing their little group to continually flick their hands across their faces. Scruffy dogs wandered across the straw mat and off the other side. "We need some refreshment," Mehdi said, clicking his fingers at someone. A teenage girl instantly appeared with a tray of porcelain pots and plastic cups. "This is *tuak*," Mehdi said, "rice wine."

Turnball laughed. "Rice wine? How do you order that in a restaurant? 'Today we have a fine white rice or, if you prefer, a tasty brown wild rice with a faint hint of water buffalo and bare feet.'" The others looked at each other, not having a clue what he was talking about. Rachel stared at him in smoldering rage. But the wine was good. Chilled. Sweet. It went down fast. Turnball had another. And another.

The Chief went away. They probably told him why, but Turnball was no longer paying attention. The rice wine was doing a number on him. The Chief returned, dressed in braided vest and fringed skirt of palm leaves, with a headdress of tall, thin, feathers. He carried a shield and a machete. Somebody banged on a gong and the Chief started slapping the machete against the shield and making jerky dance steps.

Turnball cackled. "You're freaking ferocious, old man! My head's shrinking just looking at you!"

"Shut up, Richard," Rachel snarled.

Turnball filled his cup one more time. The Chief danced away, as gracefully as a stiff-in-the-knees 80-year-old can dance. "Good stuff!" Turnball shouted. "You can dance with my stars anytime."

The teenage girl returned, wearing a knee-length straw dress covered with braided decorations and random sequins, wearing another feather headdress. Again with the gong. She flicked her hands and twitched her hips and swirled to the music. *Nice butt*, Turnball noted, *and probably other good things hidden under that ethnic nun outfit*. He took another shot of wine.

Things became jumbled. He remembered Mehdi helping him outside to pee in the bushes. Somebody brought bowls of roasted chicken and sticky rice. They ate with their hands. He peed again, and when he came back several women were squatting in front of Rachel offering her reed baskets and wooden bracelets and sandals. Mehdi had disappeared, but left behind the pot of wine. *Great guy*, Turnball said to himself. *Really great guy*.

"Are you interested in these?" Rachel asked.

"Wha—?"

She showed him a blow pipe with darts. A machete. An imitation shrunken head carved from a small wooden block. Turnball took the blow pipe and started spitting darts at the wall. They hit with a satisfying plunk.

Then he woke up, surprised. The veranda was deserted. He started to get to his feet but a hand on his shoulder pushed him back down. Mehdi. "Here is a blanket. You should sleep here."

"Where's Rach?"

"Women guests sleep with one of the families."

"Tha-that's not fair."

"It is our way."

Turnball grunted and stood. "Well, screw that." He walked along the veranda yelling, "Rach! Where are you?"

No response, which made him angrier. This was supposed to be their weekend together. Not a goddamn slumber party with a bunch of jungle sisters.

Mehdi led him back to the straw mat. He suddenly had a headache. And was tired. Mehdi handed him a pillow.

He woke to the sound of music. The veranda was deserted. Out in the yard there was a group of teenagers around a small bonfire, smoking and talking softly, laughing among themselves. Turnball pulled himself up and walked out to join them.

He recognized the girl that had danced for them. A white T-shirt and tight jeans proved that she had been hiding things under that native dress.

The group broke up as he approached. But the teen-age girl remained, waiting for him. He gave her his best smile. *If you're not near the one you love, love the one you're near*, he told himself. He pulled out some dollars, just in case that was the way things were done out here.

◊◊◊

They woke Rachel with a fuss. "Missy, Missy, your man gone." Early morning sunlight came through the windows slats. "Gone?" Rachel asked in confusion, still half asleep. "What do you mean, 'gone'?"

"Last night, he leave house to pee-pee. No come back."

Rachel slowly sat up, her back sore from sleeping on the hard floor. "I don't understand."

Mehdi knelt in front of her. "It seems Richard got up in the middle of the night to pee outside the compound. In the jungle. He seems to be lost."

"Jungle bad place," said the woman who had been jabbering at her.

Rachel stood up. "Wh—what can I do?"

Mehdi smiled to reassure her. "Wait here. We are looking everywhere. You should not go into the jungle. We will be asking the authorities for their help. Have breakfast with the women and stay here."

She stayed. But nothing happened. Mehdi appeared around noon and told her that she should go back with the canoe. Ali would be at the landing waiting for her. There was nothing she could do, and she would be better off back at the resort. Rachel protested but finally understood no one wanted her here, as if she were getting in the way.

She went back to the resort and waited. For a week. But she had to go back to her job. Ali came to say goodbye, accompanied by a policeman who apologized and said there was no news but they would contact her when they had something to report. He took the details of Turnball's employer in Singapore and family in the USA and her contact numbers in Singapore.

◊◊◊

There was no further news. As if Richard was forgotten. He had walked into the jungle, probably still intoxicated, and disappeared from the face of the earth.

Then one day, Rachel's secretary brought a small box into her office. "A messenger left this for you."

Rachel took the box. There was no writing on it, no mailing address, no return address.

"Are you sure this is for me? Who brought it in? UPS? DHL? The post office?"

The secretary shrugged. "Just a boy wearing a motorcycle helmet. He said it was for you, then left."

Rachel tore off the brown wrapping paper. She used a metal letter opener to pry open the wooden lid. Rachel recognized Richard's face, even though it had a dark brown tinge. It was shrunken to the size of a small grapefruit, with stitching through the eyes, nose, and mouth— the perfect artifact of a forgotten craft.

Rachel fainted.

Getting There

THE ELECTRONIC DISPLAY read Flight 444, but the destination was not listed. The queue inched forward at the pace of boredom. The counter attendant rarely looked up, too busy with paperwork and punching keys on the computer. She exchanged a few angry words with a customer now and then, but the client always accepted the boarding pass, then wandered away, seemingly not having a clue where to go next.

Edward bounced on his toes in anxiety and leaned out to measure the progress of the line in front of him, then stretched upward to look over the heads to see if he could see what was going on at the counter. He finally spent most of his time looking both left and right to gauge the movement of the queues parallel to his.

The intriguing part, as far as he was concerned, was that he didn't recall coming to the airport. He remembered leaving the house, dumping his briefcase on the front passenger seat of the car, taking Route 412 as usual, then driving up the access ramp to Interstate 78 East. But he couldn't remember driving to the airport and now he had forgotten where he had parked. Short-term or long -term parking? He searched his coat pockets and his slacks for the parking ticket but couldn't find one. Then he realized that he had forgotten his briefcase, too. He didn't have his airline ticket, either. For that matter, he couldn't remember where he was going. And he didn't remember packing any luggage.

He decided he had better go back outside to look for his car, recover his briefcase and see if he had packed a suitcase. But as he stepped out of line, a burly airline employee in a red jacket and bad toupee rudely pushed him back into the queue. "You can't leave," the man yelled. "Keep in line. Don't hold everyone up by getting outta line."

Edward held up his hands, palms out, to calm the man down. "I need to go back out," he began to explain, "To find—"

"There is no going back out."

"You don't understand—"

"Maybe *you* don't understand."

Edward blinked. He definitely did not understand.

"You're dead. You have no place to go except wherever this line goes."

"I'm dead?"

"Apparently you are both dead and hard of hearing."

"But . . . if I'm dead . . . where am I going?"

"To your final destination."

"Where is that?"

"How in the hell do I know? I just work here."

Edward did not like the first part of that sentence but didn't want to call it to the man's attention. His instincts, and everything he had heard and read, didn't indicate that there would be a lot of cursing in heaven.

"Am I on my way to purgatory, perhaps?" he asked, his voice calm but hopeful.

The burly employee glared at him, giving Edward the impression that the man thought Edward was an idiot. "Just stay in line," was all he said, walking away.

Edward tried to think back about the drive to work this morning, but nothing came to him. He was also surprised by his lack of emotion about being dead. Shouldn't he be feeling sorry for himself, or at least a bit disappointed? But nothing along that line surfaced. Then he thought that he should probably think about his family, his friends, his co-workers, and everybody he had apparently just left behind. But nothing came to him on that, either. Maybe later, he told himself, once he got all of this settled and straightened out.

It took forever, metaphorically speaking, to arrive at the counter. Without looking up, the red-faced woman, also in a red jacket and with a bad hairdo, said, "Edward Streeter."

"How do you know that? I didn't say anything yet."

"It's in the computer. Edward Streeter, 1020 Sycamore Avenue, Topsburg, Pennsylvania."

"Oh. No. That's not my address," Edward said, his spirits suddenly lifting. "Maybe you have the wrong Edward Streeter."

"Are you or are you not Edward Streeter?"

"I am, but maybe there is another Edward Streeter, and you have the wrong one. Edward P. Streeter. Maybe I shouldn't be dead yet."

The woman tapped on the computer. "The system doesn't give a middle initial."

"Maybe the system needs updating."

"You just got here and now you're telling us how to run the system?"

"I just think you may be making an error. This could be . . . serious . . . for me, I mean."

The woman looked back down at her computer. "According to the records, it wouldn't make any difference which Edward Streeter you were." With that, she stamped a boarding pass, initialed it, and handed it to him. "There's a flight delay. Technical failure. Just wait here in the terminal until you hear us call your flight."

"How long do you think the delay will be?"

"Who knows? An hour or two, maybe a day or two. Who knows?"

"If it is going to be that long, shouldn't I get a lunch and a hotel voucher, or something?"

"It's an act of God. Nothing we can do about it."

"I thought you said it was a technical failure?"

"Technically, it's an act of God."

Edward sighed in despair. This was getting totally out of hand. "I want to talk to your manager."

The woman smiled for the first time that morning. "You're kidding, right?"

"Can you at least tell me where this flight is going?"

She ignored the question, but reached into a drawer to pull out a booklet of vouchers. "Here's a coupon for lunch and coffee. You can use it anywhere in the terminal. Please step aside now," she said, dismissing him as she leaned around him to shout, "Next, please."

He walked away in a daze. This was all becoming too much for him. Out of habit, he thought of calling his office, but remembered that his cell phone was in his briefcase, wherever that was. Maybe he could borrow a phone, but everyone inside the terminal seemed to be in a foul, foul mood, so he didn't dare ask. Anyway dead people probably couldn't call back to their offices.

He saw a bookshop: Cowshed & Ignoble. All the shelves were filled with the same book. A James Patterson novel. The sign above the cash register said: *No Returns—No Refunds.*

He wandered off until he spotted a coffee shop named "Blackholepennies." Not encouraging. But it was the only food outlet he could see. The young girl behind the cash register, dressed in a red blouse and green apron, with a fairly decent perm, yawned and asked, "A latté? A café latté? A crème latté? A cappuccino? A decaf? A serré? An allongé? A Viennois? A Noisette? An espresso? A petit noir? A—"

"A latté, thank you."

"We are out of lattés."

"Then why did you mention it?"

"Company rules. We have to read you the entire menu."

"How many coffees do you have on the menu?"

"I don't know. I've never make it to the end. You guys keep interrupting me."

"A regular coffee, please," Edward said.

"What size do you want? We have tiny, very small, small, grandé, regular, medium, large medium—"

"Regular," Edward said quickly, then added, "What do you have to eat? I am dying of hunger."

"If you don't know it yet, you're already dead. You can no longer die from hunger."

"Thanks for the good news, but do you have anything to eat or not?"

"No."

Edward handed her the coupon for the coffee, but she waved it away. "Go sit down. I'll bring it to your table."

He found an empty table, noticing that everyone in the café was sitting by themselves, as if no one knew anybody else. Which led him to the deep (and scary) thought that maybe everyone here, or at least the customers, had all just died, too. He leaned over to talk to the woman at the next table. She was quite attractive but apparently in a bad mood. "Can I ask you a question?" Edward asked politely.

The woman stared at him coldly, then said, "Drop dead."

"Apparently I already have," Edward said, with a polite smile. "I just wanted—"

The woman turned away from him to discourage further conversation.

The waitress brought the coffee to the table. "Two dollars," she said.

"I have a coupon."

"We don't take coupons."

"The woman at the counter said—"

"We don't take coupons."

Edward pulled out his wallet to count the money he had. One hundred dollars in tens and twenties. Depending how long he was going to be dead, a hundred dollars was not going to go very far. He happily found two dollars in his pants pocket to give to the girl.

"No tip?" she said sarcastically.

He had just about had enough of everybody in this damned place. He handed her the coupon. "Maybe you'll find someplace to use it."

She accepted it but walked off in a huff. To his surprise (or maybe not) the coffee was cold, and stale. He waved to a boy in a red shirt, red bow tie, with a green apron and buzz cut, who was wiping the adjacent tables with a dirty cloth. The boy wiped his hands with the cloth and came over to Edward's table.

"This coffee's cold. And stale," Edward said.

"The machine's broken. The coffee is two days old."

"I just paid two dollars for it."

"Didn't you have a coupon?"

"Yeah, but she wouldn't take it."

The boy laughed, "You've just been scammed. Happens a lot around here."

"And you think that's funny?"

"Funnier than cleaning dirty tables for eternity."

"I'm going to report you both."

"To who?"

"To your manager."

Like the woman at the ticket counter, the boy smiled as if Edward had just told him a really good joke. "Right. Why don't you do that?"

"I see no reason why I have to take this shoddy treatment."

The boy picked up Edward's cup of coffee and starting wiping the table beneath it. "Is your flight number 444? I just heard them announcing last call. You might want to hurry out to your gate."

"I don't even know which gate it is," Edward complained.

"You gotta go through security first. That's across the hall. You can ask them which gate."

"Security?"

"You're in an airline terminal. What'd you expect?"

"I didn't expect any of this."

The boy rolled his eyes. "Who did?"

Contrary to the check-in counter, the security line was moving fast, mainly because very few people had any purses, carry-ons (or briefcases). But everyone still had to take off their coats or jackets, their shoes and their belts. They also had to empty their pockets, putting their loose change, billfolds, and whatever else into a separate tray. And even with all that, some were herded off into private rooms for more thorough examinations.

A tall man in another red uniform, totally bald, with hair coming out of his ears and nose, patted Edward down, apparently satisfied that he was not trying to hide anything.

"May I dare ask what you are looking for?" Edward said. "I assume everyone in here is dead. And you're still worried about terrorists? What dangerous items could a dead person be smuggling onto an airplane?"

"You don't know, do you?" the man asked in surprise.

"No," Edward responded honestly. "I don't have a clue."

"Bibles, crucifixes, Saint Christopher medals, rosaries, that kind of thing."

"That's . . . contraband?"

"Damn right, pardon my expression. Some people have those things on them or in their clothes and expect to bring them along, as if that stuff is going to do them any good from this point on. But we ain't gonna let that happen. Too late now. They had their chance before they got here. If someone looks really suspicious, we take them into the private rooms for body searches."

"Body searches? People have Saint Christopher medals in their mouths? Or up their—"

"They don't do it. Their family does. They're on their death bed and somebody, meaning well of course, hangs a crucifix around their neck or wraps a rosary around their wrist, or plants a Bible in their clothes. Those crazy Italian families will stuff a saint's medal into their mouth or jam it up their ass, whatever. Damned Irish are the worst. They won't repent until the last half hour, and then ask God to forgive them and grab for anything they can find that might help. There's all hell to pay around here, pun not intended, if we miss something, believe you me."

Edward gathered his jacket, belt, and shoes, glad that his family was not very religious. The truth be told, he really didn't have a family. Divorced, his kids with their mother, his parents already dead (would he see them soon?), his siblings off doing their own thing. Would they (whoever was running this place) let him watch his own funeral? It would be interesting to see who came. He would have to find somebody to ask about that.

The loading onto the plane was chaos. The walkway leading from the terminal to the plane was a mile long and zigzagged at sharp angles every ten feet. Seating was first come, first served, and everybody was in a surly mood, fighting not to get stuck in a middle seat. Edward found himself being pushed toward the rear section of the plane, then was jammed into a middle row that had eight seats.

A really fat lady, with her bare arms as long and as fat and as wrinkled as elephant trunks, sat down on his left, appropriating that arm rest. She smelled like re-cycled baby powder. A very, very large man in a leath-er motorcycle jacket with a bushy beard and tattoos on both his forehead and neck sat down on his right, taking the other arm rest. He smelled like burned gasoline, bur-ritos, and stale sweat. A mother and father with a cranky two-year old sat at the far end of the row. Edward leaned back in his seat and closed his eyes, totally enveloped in despair. *"Oh, please, God, let this flight be quick,"* he whis-pered, quite conscious that this was the first time he had prayed in years. A small boy sitting behind him began kicking the back of his seat. *Kick, kick, kick.* Edward prayed harder.

The flight preparations were quick. No one bothered with seat belt announcements, or talked about raised tray tables or portable electronics or flight time. People were still walking up and down the aisles when the plane lurched away from the gate. It taxied out, then farther out, turning here and then there, onto another taxiway. The fat lady was already snoring. The motorcycle man farted, saying, "There, that's better."

Edward suddenly had the sneaking suspicion that the plane was going to drive to wherever they were going as the plane just kept taxiing on and on and on. Then it shut down.

The pilot came over the intercom. "Sorry folks, but due to congestion, we're going to be parked here for a while. Please remain in your seats, as we don't know when we'll be given the green light. Oh, and I've been advised that the toilets are broken, so please don't bother trying to use them. But I expect we will only be here for a short while."

A flight attendant hurried up the aisle, and Edward waved at her, "Miss? Miss? Can we get something to drink? Or eat?"

She stopped. "What would you like?"

"A Coke?"

"We don't have any."

"A beer?"

"We don't have any."

"Water?"

"We don't have any."

"What do you have?"

She laughed. "Nothing." Then walked away, never to be seen again.

Eventually the lights went off and the air conditioning shut down. Somebody said he had to pee and somebody told him to use an empty bottle. Then Edward's motorcycle companion got up to start kicking at the toilet door, saying he had to shit and he sure as hell wasn't going to do it in the aisle. He finally got the door open but then it wouldn't close. But he shit anyway, with his blue jeans around his ankles, smiling at everyone watching him. He fluttered his fingers at Edward, as if they were buddies. A handful of other folks decided to take their turn after he came back to his seat. The smell quickly became toxic, waves of transparent fumes radiating down the aisles.

Edward told himself he could hold it. He could hold it, damn it. He could hold it. But then he couldn't, so he got up to pee in the fouled bathroom, which made him even sicker than he already was. He ran back to his seat, desperately trying not to vomit.

He finally fell asleep, or passed out, he wasn't sure which. The motion of the plane woke him. He was overjoyed. They were taking off. But the pilot came back on the intercom to announce they were going back to the terminal as there were several red warning lights coming on in the cockpit that they could not ignore. They would have to change planes.

Edward was too drained to react.

Then the pilot added, "When you return to the terminal, you will need to check in at the ticket counter again as your current boarding passes will no longer be valid. You will also have to go back though security before you can re-board. We are very sorry about these delays but, from all of us on board, we wish you a good day." There was a moment of silence, then the pilot cracked up in laugher before he turned off the intercom.

In that instant, Edward understood: The airport *was* his destination.

Dead Man Breathing

I SAT ON THE RIDGE waiting for the sun to come up. Old Henry nuzzled me on the shoulder as if anxious to get moving. The old pack mule was probably tired of being hobbled up and just wanted to move his legs and wander off to somewhere to scrounge for food. On the other hand, even a dumb animal could sense there was too much death in the camp behind us and it was time to get the hell out of there.

Going or staying didn't matter. I was a dead man breathing. The water hole smelled putrid. The standing water was opaque white and brackish and tasted sour. It made me vomit if I drank too much. Even scrawny old Henry refused to drink out of it.

Great choice: stay here and poison myself or pack up the stupid mule and move on—into an endless desert that had no water. Only burned-out cactus and rock. Red rocks, brown rocks, and occasional black rocks, all scorched by the searing sun. It didn't matter in which direction I went. Just more of the same.

And that damn bunch of raggedy-ass Indians was still out there. Probably watching me right now. Waiting to surprise me. I had more guns than one man could use, three pistols and three rifles, but could only shoot one at a time. Maybe two pistols at a time, but how do you aim

141

when you're shooting two pistols and a bunch of damn Indians are swarming around you? I ain't ever tried and don't want to find out.

How'd I get here?

It didn't start out bad.

John Rogers had a contract to move one hundred head of cattle out of El Paso to Fort Washington, north of Del Rio. Said he needed another hand. He had a good rider named Jameson and a half-breed Indian who claimed to know the territory like the back of his hand. He even had a Chinese cook called Chan who was going to drive the chuck wagon, then move on to San Antonio to find a job.

Four riders with a well-supplied chuck wagon with a good cook ought to be able to handle a hundred head of cattle. But getting them from El Paso to Fort Washington might be a hard effort. "Ain't hardly enough grass out there to keep 'em fed," I said.

Rogers took off his hat to wipe his brow. The top half of his forehead was white from where the hat protected him from the sun. "We don't need to get them there fat," he said. "We just need to get them there. They're the Army's problem after that."

So I signed on. I was sick of El Paso. Been there a month. Too many cheats at the gambling tables and not enough new whores in the sporting houses. And I was never cut out for working in a city. Too many people. Too many rules.

The only hesitation I had was when Rogers said we were going to cross the Apache Mountains.

"It's pretty well quieted down out there now," Rogers claimed. "A few roving bands here and there but they're getting them rounded up."

"Who says?"

Montés, the half breed, was standing beside Rogers. He spit on the ground and smiled at me like the smile hurt his face. "You 'fraid of a couple old 'paches that don' know when to quit?"

He was short and stocky with skin the color of dark wood, with a nice scar running from the corner of his left eye brow to his upper lip as if somebody tried to cut half his head off. He had a soiled bandanna wrapped around his forehead that looked like it hadn't been washed in the past two years.

"Four men and a cook riding a hundred cows into Apache country might make a tempting target to a couple of old Apaches that don't know when to quit," I said.

Montés spit on the ground again and turned away from me. "We don' need you. Three of us can handle it."

I looked over at Rogers. "Who's running the show? You or him?"

"We need you, Marcus. You're a good cowhand and you can shoot. I've seen you do it."

"Do you need to go through those mountains?"

Rogers shrugged and stared at the countryside at the edge of town. "It cuts off fifty miles and the valleys between are flat with a few watering holes. With a little luck we can make it to Fort Washington with all hundred head."

"And all four of ours, too?"

"That's the plan."

◊◊◊

So off we went. At the break of dawn. Out of the cattle yards north of El Paso. Rogers, Jameson, and I counted the cows, crowding them into a herd. They bawled and bellowed, and acted frisky and ornery, still fresh with energy, but finally settled into a loose, ragged file.

Montés rode far in front of us as if he had nothing to do with getting this operation started. Chan came rolling out of town in the chuck wagon, lashing the two mules with his whip, waving and yelling as he hurried to catch up, the pots and pans clanging against the side boards.

The cows were plodding along straight and placid, so I dropped back to ride beside Chan. He was chubby and cheerful and looked to be the talkative type, which might be a nice change from the usual taciturn cowpokes that I rode with. Within two days of any ride, ten words around a campfire in the evening marked you as a social animal. "You sure you're riding with the right crowd?" I asked with a smile.

"You Malcus?"

"I'm Marcus," I replied, correcting him.

"Tha's wha' I said. Malcus."

He was dressed funny. A white cotton jacket with buttons and a high collar, floppy pants, and a round hat that looked like the ones the cooks in some fancy restaurant might wear. His rickety old wagon sure as hell was not a fancy restaurant, and we didn't yet know how well he could cook.

"You know you're going to San Antonio the long way," I kidded.

"Need to work. Nothin' flee in this country."

Flee or flea? Big difference. I went with free, which made me laugh. "Tell me about it," I said. "Where you from?"

"China. I Chinaman."

"I can see that. From where in China?"

"Why? You know China?"

"No, I was just making conver—"

Rogers yelled at me, pointing at a cow and her calf wandering off by themselves into a small arroyo. Already? This might turn out to be a long trip.

◊◊◊

Damned if Chan couldn't cook. He was good. Real good. He made bacon and beans worth farting about. And spaghetti. I never had spaghetti on a ride before. With meat sauce. He called them noodles. But we knew they was spaghetti. Jameson had never heard the word *noodles* before.

Chan even found the way into Montés' heart. The two of them would ride out in front of the herd all day scouting the route and looking for a camp site for the evening. Then, while they were waiting for us, Chan would go out searching for snakes and lizards and finding wild onions and grasshoppers, and cactus pears.

But he was smart enough, in the beginning, not to tell us what we was eating. He'd have those snakes and lizards stripped and cut up and boiled or grilled by the time we arrived and mix all of it in with beans and toasted biscuits. Montés would eat his without the beans. Just the onions and cactus pears.

Then about the fourth night, Jameson asked, "What is this white stuff? It's damned good."

"Lattlesnake," Chan said.

"What the hell is lattlesnake?"

Montés grinned at him and answered for Chan, "Rattlesnake. He means rattlesnake."

Jameson went as white as the pallid strips of snake on his plate, then rose to his feet to walk outside of the fire light to vomit in the bushes.

Chan had a horrified look on his face. "You no want me to cook lattlesnake no more?"

Rogers and I exchanged looks. We knew it wasn't bothering Montés any and it sure as hell wasn't bothering either one of us. Rogers shook his head and spit on the ground. "Man's gotta eat," he said.

◊◊◊

The trouble started at the end of the first week. Something, or someone, spooked the herd. Rogers was riding the late night watch and said he heard nothing, absolutely nothing, but all of a sudden the herd took off like someone stuck a hot branding iron straight up their collective asses.

It took us at least two miles before we rounded them up and settled them down, and we didn't have a clue where we were. Chan and his wagon caught up to us at dawn and treated us to a well-deserved breakfast.

The morning count said we lost ten cows.

We spent the morning looking for them. But not a trace. Another day wasted.

One of Chan's mules disappeared the next night. "I had them hobbled," Chan protested. "Hobbled good. Andrew really tight, 'cause he like to wander off. Old Henry not so much. He too old and want to rest at night."

"You named your mules?" Jameson asked in surprise.

"Sure, I name my mules. How I talk to them if I don't know their names?"

"They're just . . . mules."

"They work belly hard. They should have names."

Jameson walked off muttering to himself. But Rogers, Montés, and I looked at one another. We knew something was going on out there at night.

"Can you pull the wagon with only one mule?" Rogers asked Chan.

"Belly hard. Belly, belly hard. Old Henry belly old. Maybe you give me a cow to pull, too."

"You're gonna hitch a cow and mule to pull the wagon?"

"You got better idea?"

Which slowed us down further. The cow and mule were not a great team. And the country was getting harder. We had to cut back our distance per day to let Chan and his badly matched eight legged crew catch up.

Montés disappeared the third night. Jameson was out riding watch. The half breed volunteered to stand watch around the camp while Rogers and I settled into our blankets. Chan was cleaning his pots and pans before climbing into his wagon to sleep.

In the morning, everything about Montés was gone: His blankets, his saddle bags, his horse, and his guns.

"This ain't right," Jameson said, visibly upset.

"But where he go?" Chan asked, bewildered.

I was the one who said it. "I think he just changed sides."

Rogers nodded, not speaking.

"D—do we know how to get there from here? To Fort Washington, I mean?" Jameson asked.

"More or less," Rogers said.

"Less than more," I added.

"Just as bad going back," Rogers said.

I shrugged. "They're waiting out there for us, either way we go."

Jameson did not like that comment. He apparently hadn't figured it out yet. "They? Waiting out there for us? Who the hell is out there waiting for us?"

"One of them roving bands the Army hasn't brought in yet," I said.

"Probably," Rogers confirmed.

"And Montés just joined them?" Jameson said, red in the face.

"Probably," Rogers repeated.

"Or he cut bait and went home. Did the count and decided we were on the losing side," I said.

"So what are we gonna do?"

Rogers walked over to his horse to start saddling up, but looked back at Jameson. "Just keep on going. Only thing we *can* do."

But we had to abandon the chuck wagon. It was too risky to have Chan trundling along way behind both of us. Too exposed all by himself. So we unloaded the wagon as best we could and packed it on old Henry and formed a bare spot between the bundles for Chan to ride. Neither old Henry nor Chan were happy about it, but at least Chan understood the situation.

The pattern began to change. A handful of cows would now disappear every other night. Rogers and I decided that the Apaches were herding them off bit by bit to a main camp not far away. No point in fighting us when they could whittle us to death.

The question then became if it was too dangerous for us to ride watch at night. Another easy way to get picked off, one by one. And our patrolling around the herd wasn't doing any good; they were peeling off a half-dozen cows whenever they wanted.

"Might as well dump the whole lot and ride on," Rogers said. "We ain't gonna fulfill the contract and get paid if we show up at Fort Washington with ten cows."

"They ain't gonna let us show up with even ten cows," I said.

Jameson frowned. "What do you mean by that?"

"They want the whole bag. Our horses, guns, saddles, probably our clothes. If Montés is with them, they know what we got. And we don't even know if we're going in the right direction. We may be heading straight into the desert, on the other side of the damn mountains."

Jameson turned to Rogers, wanting him to contradict me. But he didn't. "Marcus is probably right," he said quietly.

Chan didn't say a word. He understood, aware he was caught in a situation completely out of his control. His only choice was to trust us.

"So what are we going to do?" Jameson asked.

"Cut and run," Rogers said. "We make camp tonight like we always do, but saddle up just before dawn and then get the hell out of here at first light. We stampede the cows in one direction and we ride like hell in the other."

Chan finally spoke up. "What I ride?"

"With one of us."

"What I do with ol' Henry?"

"Let him go."

"No want to do that. He be with me for long time."

Rogers shrugged. "You're choice. But we ain't waiting to pull him along. If he can't keep up, we cut him loose."

"I ride him," Chan said. "He keep up."

Roger nodded. "Like I said, your choice. But we ain't gonna wait for you."

"I pack pots and pans and food?"

I stepped in this time. I didn't think Chan was getting the message about what we were up against. "Pack only what you can squeeze into a saddlebag. I suggest food and canteens only. Tie on a pot or pan or two, but keep it light 'cause that's the only chance you have to keep up with us. Do you have a gun?"

Chan frowned. "No gun."

"Do you want one?"

"Don't know how to use."

I patted him on the shoulder with affection. He had little chance of keeping up with us, and I hated to imagine what the Apaches would do to him when they caught him. "You'd better make ol' Henry run," was all I could say.

◊◊◊

The plan almost worked.

Dawn came and we whooped and hollered and chased them cows off in a bellowing cloud of dust in a dozen different directions while we split off on another, like the devil was behind us. If you have Apaches chasing you, it's damn near the same thing.

We looked back and saw about a dozen of them Indian fellows riding like mad to push that herd back together. They were having a hard time at it, just like we hoped.

But there were three of them trailing us. Not riding hard. Just loping along, keeping sight of us.

Rogers signaled for us to slow down. We weren't gonna out run 'em, so we might was well save our horses. It was going to be a long ride.

He looked over at me and said, "Now what?"

"Keep on moving. It's gonna take a while for them fellas to rein in the herd. The three of them behind us ain't gonna attack us on their own. Maybe we can get some place safe before they get organized again."

Rogers glanced back again. "Is that Montés riding lead?"

I swung around for a good look. I recognized the stocky body and bandanna. It was Montés.

"Maybe we can bargain with him," Jameson suggested.

"Doubt it. He's chosen sides. Unless we get somewhere safe, they got the upper hand."

◊◊◊

It was my idea, so I was the one who had to do it.

We went around a bend and would be out of sight of our stalkers for a moment or two. I dismounted, pulling my rifle out of its saddle holster and ran up between some boulders for a view of the back trail. They were still coming. They picked up speed so as not to lose sight of us.

I waited until they were in range. One shot. Montés fell off his horse. The other two jumped from their horses and dove behind the rocks before I could squeeze off a second shot. These boys were good. They'd done this before.

I stayed in position a few more minutes.

Their horses stood stock still, waiting. Montés remained on the ground, not moving. Silence. A hawk screeched overhead. I hurried down from the boulders and mounted to catch up to Rogers, Jameson, and Chan.

◊◊◊

We rode through the days and exhausted our water and what little food we had. Then at night, we huddled without a campfire, frozen under our blankets, barely sleeping. Still they came. Just the two of them. Then just one of them. And then they were gone. Or so we thought.

But the desert was still endless. We might have been riding in circles. We tried to keep track of east from west and north from south, but the sun seemed to be directly overhead from mid-morning until late afternoon.

We assumed we escaped from the Indians but were now going to die in the desert. Chan was the only one who kept us going. He caught scorpions and spiders and grasshoppers, green lizards, and more rattlesnakes and started to roast them over campfires again in the evenings as we thought we were now safe from the Indians. Jameson grumbled and bitched but ate whatever Chan came up with.

Then we found the water hole. Just in time, too, as we had been out of water for two days. We drank from it, thirstily, and vomited. Chan tried to boil it but we still vomited. It was rank. Repulsive. But the only water we had.

We camped next to it, trying to decide which direction to take in the morning. Chan made a good campfire that we huddled around, nibbling on the inedibles that he came up with until we fell asleep. In the morning, our horses were gone.

"Them goddamn Indians," Jameson cursed.

"Caught up with us," Rogers said.

"Took all three horses without making a noise."

"But left ol' Henry," I said.

Jameson stared at the mule. "Not enough meat on him to eat and probably too embarrassing for even an Indian to ride."

"Wha' we do now?" Chan asked.

Rogers took off his hat to rub his forehead as if he had a headache. "Walk or fight, I guess."

I looked at the desert in front of us. "Gonna be a tough walk."

"If we stay here, we got the water hole. If Chan can keep feeding us, we can hold out for a while. Maybe they'll get tired of waiting now that they got our horses."

"Or attack us if they get bored waiting."

"We got the water, the guns and the rocks to hide behind. That makes it their move."

"Damn," Jameson said.

◊◊◊

That plan didn't work out. We lost our food supply. Jameson was on the outside edge of the fire, hiding behind some small boulders on night watch. Chan woke in the middle of the night to step out of the fire light to take a piss. A dozen arrows thunked into him. He fell to the ground in the darkness with a sigh.

Jameson went berserk, firing into the night in every direction around us. Rogers and I rolled out of our blankets, guns in hand, but stayed on the ground to keep out of Jameson's crazed line of fire as well as from any spare arrows that hadn't been used on Chan.

When Jameson finally stopped shooting (*out of ammunition?*) there was only silence. No rustling sounds in the bushes. No return fire, bullets, or arrows. Chan moaned softly in the shadows.

None of the three of us were going out to fetch him. Could be a setup. Lure us out there, then jump us and fill another one of us full of arrows. Chan was just going to have to wait until morning light.

Which seemed to take a year to come. But it finally did. No trace of our attackers. Vanished. Evaporated. Melted away into the desert. *How do they do that?*

Chan lay on the ground ten yards away, looking like a very fat porcupine with arrows substituting for quills. Making no more sounds.

We sat to collect ourselves. Everything was untouched, except for the ammunition that Jameson wasted shooting into the dark. Again, the Indians didn't bother to take old Henry. We were amazed that Jameson didn't shoot him while he was filling the night full of lead.

"Guess we should bury him," Rogers said, looking over at Chan.

"Hell of a place to be buried," I replied. "In the middle of nowhere."

Jameson walked over to look down at the body. "We bury him, we ain't gonna get him down very far. The ground's all rock and hard dirt. A coyote or some other critter is going to come along and dig him up soon as we leave here."

"We don't bury him, the sun's coming up and he's gonna start rotting real quick," Rogers said.

"We could eat him," Jameson said.

Rogers and I both turned to Jamison, stunned.

"Eat him?" I could barely force the words out of my mouth.

Jameson nudged Chan with his boot. "I got news for you. He's dead and we are now out of food. We were nearly starving in spite of what he was feeding us and I ain't scrounging around the ground looking for spiders, ants, lizards, and rattlesnakes. I don't think you guys are gonna do so either."

"I don't know if I could . . ."

Jameson leaned close as if trying to sniff him. "We gotta make up our minds real soon."

"It don't seem right to eat the cook," I said.

"I never ate Chinese before," Rogers said in a failed attempt at black humor.

"I have," I replied. "One time in 'Frisco. Noodles and all kinds of spices. Rice, too. Wasn't bad."

"We ain't got no noodles," Jameson said.

Rogers smiled in spite of himself. "I bet Chan could have come up with some spices, I mean if he was the one still alive, looking to cook one of us."

We busied ourselves extracting the arrows from his body, probably causing as much damage yanking them out as they had done going in. His pants were still down around his knees, proving that he was killed while taking a piss.

"Died with his hand on his pecker," Rogers said.

"Every man's dream," I added.

Jameson snorted. "I ain't gonna eat his pecker."

"Didn't get any arrows in it."

"Don't care. Still ain't eating it."

"We could eat ol' Henry instead," Rogers suggested.

All three of us looked over at the old mule. He was nothing but skin and bones. His ribs stuck out like slats on a barrel. He stared back at us, bleating in protest against his hobbles. I wondered if he was embarrassed because the Indians hadn't stolen him. Even raggedy-ass Indians apparently have standards.

"Ol' Henry can still carry things, you know," Jameson said. "We have Chan's pots and pans and our own bed rolls, saddles, and rifles. No point in carrying all of that while we walk around out in the desert. Ol' Henry can carry all of that, plus what water we can take, as far as he can go. Then we eat him."

He could see that Rogers and I were still not convinced. But all three of us knew we were going to die out there, one way or the other. The Indians were going to circle back to check on us to see if the desert got us, hoping to collect our guns, clothes, and whatever else we still had, without another fight.

"If we chop Chan up, Ol' Henry can also carry the leftovers when we're done," Jamison added.

"The leftovers will last longer after we cook him," Rogers volunteered, indicating that the decision had been made. But who was going to chop him up? Then cook the parts? Which parts? Or should we put him on a spit and roast him like a hog before chopping him up?

Jameson had the best knife. A Bowie. Sharp as a razor. But he was squeamish, much more than me or Rogers.

"We shoulda talked about this with Chan 'fore he died. He woulda known how to do this," Rogers said.

"Just in case we thought we were gonna eat each other?" I said. I took off my hat to wipe the sweat from my brow. It was starting to get hot and my mind was going to explode thinking about this. "Maybe we should just bury him, let him be."

Rogers nodded. "That would be the Christian thing to do."

"He wasn't a Christian," Jameson said.

"How do you know that?"

"Chinese are heathens. Everyone knows that. I say we chop him. Carve the meat off the bone. Just skip the hands and feet and ankles and everything above the neck."

"We gonna eat the organs?" Rogers asked.

"Well," Jameson said, musing out loud, "Everyone says the liver of the buffalo tastes really good and is good for you, too. And maybe the tongue. A lot of people like cow tongue."

"I ain't gonna eat no tongue. Ain't no telling where a Chinaman put his tongue," Rogers said.

"Do you think all of that will get us across this damned desert?" I asked.

"I estimate we have two hundred miles," Rogers said, looking out at the empty horizon. "We make twenty miles a day, it'll take us ten days. If we only make ten it'll take us twenty days. Gonna be touch and go, either way. Chan may or may not last. But we have ol' Henry as a backup."

I knew two hundred miles was just a guess. Rogers had no idea. Nor did I or Jameson.

"So who's gonna chop him up?" Jameson asked.

I held out my hand. "Give me the knife."

Both men looked relieved. Jamison reluctantly handed it to me. It had an elegant feel to it. Well balanced. A knife that made you want to cut something.

They both turned away as I stepped over to Chan, not wanting to watch me carve him up. I swung around, quickly cocking my Colt revolver to shoot them both in the back before they could react.

I waited until the echo of the gunshots died out in the desert vastness. I may be a dead man breathing, but I now had some extra food and more water for myself, to help me get as far as I could go. I rubbed Ol' Henry affectionately on the neck and said, "Looks like it's you and me, old partner. I'll cook 'em and you carry 'em."

East Jesus, Texas

Only a Game

ACCEPTING THE JOB of high school football coach at East Jesus, Texas, (school motto: *Don't Cross Us!*) was not a great career move. Only twelve kids came out for the team, and one of those was a girl. Given the great distances between schools, and our lack of a school bus, we had only three games scheduled, all at home. Which caused a bit of a problem, as we didn't have a football field.

Our Principal, Mr. Johnson Haywood, suggested we play the games on the school parking lot. I said that might be confusing due to the permanent white lines painted on it for the parking slots. Mr. Haywood countered my argument by pointing out that the blue lines for the handicapped slots would make a natural end zone. I won the squabble by mentioning that if we played in the parking lot, there would be no place for the spectators to park (assuming more than twelve sets of parents would come to watch the games). So we agreed to move to the field across the road, to old Mr. Detweiler's cow pasture.

Old Mr. Detweiler said he didn't mind but he had nowhere else to put the cows, so we were just gonna have to shoo them off to the far side of the pasture whenever we wanted to practice or play. Of course, that also meant that we were gonna have to shovel and clean the cow patties from the area we wanted to play on. Old Mr. Detweiler said that wasn't his problem.

The kids were more enthusiastic about clearing that field than I thought they would be. But I shoulda known they were gonna turn it into a massive manure throw. A few got to seeing how far they could hurl a cow patty. The older, dried up patties, worked best—if you used the discus technique. But, of course, a couple of kids decided to go for accuracy (wet patties work better here), and that degenerated into an all-out brawl. I didn't stop it, though, as I thought it brought the team closer together, which is important in any sport.

Equipment also turned out to be a problem. We didn't have any. But the helmet part was easily resolved. Most of the kids used their own bicycle headgear, or borrowed (or stole) their older brothers' motorcycle helmets. We painted them all purple (school colors: *The Purple Sagebrushes*) and added big white numbers on the side; any number they wanted from one to ninety-nine. Our Art/Social Studies/English teacher used this as an art project, encouraging the kids to paint on skulls and crossbones, lightning bolts, or some other menacing symbols. Margaret, our lone female, painted pink hearts and kisses on hers, which scared the hell out of everyone else on the team.

Team jerseys (Guess what? We didn't have any of those, either) turned into a community project. The players' mothers, aunts, and grandmothers got together to knit them. However, I forgot to tell them to coordinate the number on the jersey with the number on their kid's helmet, so that caused a bit of confusion when we finally got on the field. But the bigger problem was that if an opponent missed his (or her) tackle but got his (or her) fingers caught in a knitting loop, which was easy to do, the jersey would unravel all of the way to the end zone.

We compensated for this by having the women knit several backups for each game.

Shoulder pads were the real challenge. The only sporting goods store we had in a one-hundred-fifty-mile radius was Cabela's, and they mostly stocked fishing and hunting clothes, outdoor gear, camouflage tents, and hiking boots. Robbie Shelmbacher's father cobbled together a set of pads from wood slats leftover from some fencing he had done around the farm, but they came out to be kinda mean, like putting brass knuckles inside your boxing gloves. But at least he had taken the nails out.

Little Tommie Sooner came up with the best solution. His Aunt Beula's brassieres were big enough to stretch across the back of his small neck, one big cup covering each shoulder. Fill them full of old rags and cast off T-shirts and, voilà, you were ready to go.

That, too, became a team project. Unfortunately, not all of the mothers or other women had Aunt Beula's proportions. So the boys started going into the East Jesus Dollar Store (used be a 5 & 10) to pick up the bigger sizes. But they were too shy to buy them, so they started to shoplift the super sizes. The store manager, Mr. Clarendon, caught on pretty quick, but as he was a team supporter, he just sent me the bill. I tried to turn the invoices in as an expense, but got a nasty note back from the school business administrator in which she said: "You are an ugly pervert, and if you don't stop this, I will inform the school board."

What worried me more, though, was to hear the boys talking about Nylon vs. Elastane vs. Rayon vs. cotton, and padded cups vs. lift up cups and underwires. A couple of them even suggested we drive all the way into Amarillo to visit Victoria's Secret, but I told them if we were gonna drive all the way to Amarillo, we might just as well buy regular shoulder pads. All they said to that was, "Oh," kinda disappointed.

Margaret had a unique idea for thigh pads: Everyone would just tape Kotex pads across the front of their legs. But the boys became skittish on this one. They were way too timid ask their moms or sisters for their Kotex pads. Old brassieres were one thing, but Kotex pads? As it was her idea, Margaret volunteered to buy the pads for the whole team. However, on her third visit to the drugstore for another volume purchase, the pharmacist leaned over the counter to say to her, "Young lady, if I were you, I would talk to your doctor." After that, Margaret told us we would just have to use what we already had.

Practices were complicated, considering we only had twelve kids. We could practice either offense, or defense, but not both at the same time. So we brought over a few of Old Mr. Detweiler's cows. They just stood there staring at us blankly, not quite understanding what they were supposed to do, but they gave us something to run around, like blocking dummies. Occasionally one of them skittered, knocking down a kid or two, which was as close as we ever got to full contact.

The first game, against Moses, Texas, (school motto: *Watch Our People Go!*) came a little sooner that I would have liked. However, I was relieved to see they weren't any better equipped than we were. We managed to get yard lines painted on old Mr. Detweiler's field, cobbled together two field goals, and chased away those cows that thought they were gonna get to play. Then we wheeled out a portable blackboard to act as the scoreboard, and whistled for the game to begin.

The Moses half back nearly ran the opening kickoff all the way back on us, but Margaret stopped him cold on the twenty yard line. He jumped up and ran off the field and wouldn't come back, yelling that the kid who just tackled him was wearing lipstick.

I called a quick time out and told Margaret, to paraphrase the line from the old movie, "There's no lipstick in football." She wiped it off, but glared across the field to yell at their halfback, "I'll still kick your ass!" He refused to come back out for the rest of the game.

On the next play, their other half back made a neat run around our end, but slipped on a fresh cow patty that we had somehow overlooked and slid out through the sidelines, taking out the row of folding chairs the Moses supporters were sitting on. The referee wanted to run the play over again, but Mr. Haywood argued that that was our well known "Defecation Defense" and that the play should stand. Their coach was so stunned by the argument that he couldn't even respond, so the play stood.

Moses was so discouraged by the call they wasted the next two plays and we took over the ball. Margaret knocked their guard on his butt, allowing little Tommie Sooner to scoot through the opening and run ten yards before anyone could catch him. He was the only one who noticed that one of the cows had come back onto the field, and he darted around the cow, just like at practice. All three Moses defensive backs didn't see the old cow standing there and ran smack into its side, knocking it over as they sprawled across it. Old Mr. Detweiler happened to be watching the game and came out bellowing about him not agreeing to any "cow tippling" and that everyone "should just get the hell off my field."

The game was over. But the referee ruled that little Tommie Sooner had scored before the game was called, so it was East Jesus 6, Moses 0. Our first win.

The other coach was angry but rational. He suggested we might as well go inside and play basketball, even though it was a bit early in the season. They had driven all this way and it was a shame to waste the day. As I was going to be our basketball coach, too, I thought it was a reasonable suggestion. But I took Margaret aside before the game, as she was going to be our starting center, to tell her there was no lipstick in boys' basketball, either. She made a face and asked, "When we gonna get to a sport that has lipstick in it?"

I patted her gently on the shoulder and said, "I think you're gonna get there real soon, but I ain't gonna be coaching it."

We canceled the rest of the football season after that, both games, as we no longer had a field to play on. But the basketball season went well. We kept the cows out of the gym and won more than half our games. Margaret even got a full basketball scholarship, although she was sorely disappointed when she found out that it was just for the girls' team. I gave her a tube of lipstick as a going away present.

Rodeo

AS FAR AS ANYONE KNEW, Old Gus Dingby had only two interests in life: talking rodeo and spitting tobacco. And if you got him wound up talking rodeo, you were in imminent danger of getting a fair amount of 'baccy juice on your shirt, your jeans, and maybe your face. If you were smart enough to back off a respectable distance, you still risked getting ugly black stains on your boots and pant cuffs.

Knowing this, the entire bunch of us stepped back a little, trying to estimate his current spitting distance (he was losing range with age) as we trailed him through the maze of cattle pens, looking at the bulls. Even some of them eyed him through the metal bars, banging their horns against the railings as if daring him to spit in their direction.

But Gus knew his rodeo, and we were his captive audience this afternoon. The handful of kids following me had signed up to ride these bulls in tonight's East Jesus High School Annual Rodeo. Judging from the look on their faces, after listening to Gus, the romance of bull riding was losing some of its glamour.

"You're gonna get hurt ridin' bulls (*spit*). It's not *if* you're gonna get hurt (*spit*), or *when* you're gonna get hurt (*spit*). You're just damn well gonna get hurt (*spit*).

You're riding a two-ton bull who's already pissed that he is caged up in these pens (*spit*), and now you got the balls to sit on his back and think you're gonna stay there (*double spit*)? Ain't gonna happen (*spit*)."

Gus was oblivious to the effect he was having. "Once he throws you as far as he can throw you (*spit*), he's gonna try to stomp on you (*spit*). Or maybe stick a horn so far up your butt that it's gonna come outta your mouth." This last statement merited a *Hoeeey* spit—a massive, gooey, smelly load that cratered the dirt and threw sawdust at our feet.

Even the bulls edged away from that load. A couple of the boys hurried over to the pens to inhale the relief of fresh cow patties. Gus had to yank out his tobacco pouch to reload.

Being the football, basketball, baseball and part-time track coach at East Jesus High School somehow qualified me to be the conscripted staff volunteer for this event. Most of these kids were reared on farms and ranches where cows and bulls were part of the neighborhood, and most had ridden horses all their life, quite often bareback, so they knew the risks of riding large four-legged animals. But none of them had ever ridden an animal this big, this agile, this mobile, or this hostile. With one exception, they were all sophomores or freshmen. The juniors and seniors who rode bulls last year were excused from this orientation session.

I felt I had to speak up to ease the tension. "None of the kids got hurt last year, did they, Gus?"

"Nothing serious (*spit*). A couple broken arms (*spit*). A dislocated shoulder (*spit*), or two. A couple of 'em got stepped on. Busted leg (*spit*). That kinda thing. Everybody's wearing helmets and them Kevlar vests nowadays, so no head injuries or broken ribs." Gus spit this last comment out in obvious disdain, as if only girly boys wore helmets or Kevlar vests, or worried about the little things, like broken ribs. His face said *these kids are getting soft, you know what I mean?*

"You're gonna walk us through the procedures in the chute, then talk about some technique, right? About staying on and getting off the bull?" I asked.

Old Gus snorted as if I had just said the funniest thing in the world. I was afraid for a moment that some tobacco juice was going to spit out through his nose. "Ain't none of them gonna stay on very long (*spit*) and they gonna find their own way off easy enough (*spit*)."

I was tempted to tell Gus he wasn't being helpful, but I held back. Getting community volunteers was difficult, and Gus was the best known *former* bull rider in four counties. The word was that over the years, the bulls had broken every bone in his body multiple times. And he looked like it: His bowed legs were crooked and stiff, his narrow arms stuck out at awkward angles, and his bony shoulders sloped downward, left to right. He was the poster boy for riding rodeos way too long. "Shall we go over to the chute and practice the set up?" I suggested.

"Yeah, let's do that," Gus said, a gleam in his eye.

He had a tired old cow waiting for us in the arena chute. Her relationship to a menacing bull was in form and cowhide only. She was as calm as a dead tree, happy to be safe in a pen where she was being fed now and then. Old Gus had brought her in to be sure that nobody was going to get hurt during this walk through. The bull rope was already wrapped around the cow's chest, with the metal ball dangling at the bottom. It banged against the side of the chute when the old girl shifted weight. The flank strap was also strapped around her hind quarters, just to make her look official. In spite of his sarcasm, Gus was taking his responsibilities seriously.

"Who wants to set in first?" he asked.

Surprisingly, everyone's hand went up. There would be some weird-ass excuses later tonight when the real event started, but right now nobody was gonna back down from getting on top of a worn-out old cow in front of their classmates. Welcome to the world of teenagers.

Gus surveyed them, then picked the smallest one, little Tommie Sooner. I couldn't judge if he was being mean or helpful. "You, the little guy, get up here."

Little Tommie smiled as if he had just won the lottery. He accepted the Kevlar vest and traded his cowboy hat for the helmet, then scrambled over the railing to settle on the back of the cow.

"You got a glove?"

Tommie held up his right hand to show off a well-used thick leather glove. He probably got it from an older brother or uncle who spent some time around rodeos.

"You know what you're doing?"

Little Tommie wrapped his gloved hand around the bull rope and pounded it into a tight grip that eventually looked like a five-fingered knot around the rope. Somebody had been coaching him, or he had watched a lot of local television.

"And your other hand?"

Little Tommie knew what Gus wanted to see. He waved his left hand high over his head.

"You know that if you slap or even touch the bull with that hand while you're riding, you're disqualified (*spit*). No score (*spit*). You might as well just get off the bull and go home. You just wasted your time (*spit*). And ours (*spit*)."

Tommie smiled and waved his free hand in Old Gus's face. That hand was not going to touch this cow or any bull he might sit on later tonight.

"One of you other guys get down there and open the chute," Gus ordered. "But before you do, I want every one of you to look at the barrel in the middle of the arena floor. After you get throwed off, either this afternoon from this old cow, or tonight from the bulls, I want you to run and jump into that damn barrel. Just hide there until the clowns tell you to come out. If you have any luck tonight, one of you might get bumped around like a ride in an amusement park 'til the bull gets bored with it. Now, one of you open this chute (*spit*)."

Ronnie Prentice jumped down to grab the rope tied to the chute's gate, and pulled hard. The gate swung wide open. The old cow looked out at the floor of the arena and chewed her cud. It didn't interest her.

"Kick her," Old Gus yelled. Tommie Sooner kicked. But, as he didn't have spurs, his little legs didn't make much of an impact. The sagged-out old cow glanced back at him in annoyance, but didn't budge. If cows could roll their eyes, she would have rolled them in derision at little Tommie's futile efforts.

Old Gus swore under his breath and told Ronnie Prentice to close the gate. "Next," he said. "If she ain't gonna budge, we might as well let everyone have a quick sit-on. At least that will get you started," he added, waving at the tall student standing behind me.

Margaret took off her cowboy hat to put on the helmet.

Gus stared at her, lost for words, then finally sputtered, "You're a girl."

"Yes, I am," Margaret confirmed.

"You're just a damned girl."

"That's what my Pa says all the time, too. 'You're just a damned girl.' He told my Ma he would have paid her a hundred dollars on the spot if she had had a boy—and she told him to stick the hundred dollars up his ass as she was not about to try again."

"Girls can't ride bulls."

"Who says?"

"Everybody says."

"Show it to me written."

"She's right," I said. "There's nothing in the rules that says girls can't ride bulls."

"Well, shit, there oughta be. Girls barrel race. They don't ride bulls."

"Did that last year. I wanna ride bulls this year," Margaret said.

Margaret was the one exception I mentioned earlier. She was now a senior, and I didn't have the time, or patience, to tell Gus that Margaret was a mainstay on our football team, the star of our boys' basketball team, and our best pitcher during the baseball season. So I just motioned her to climb on our bovine buddy, rope in, and raise her free hand. Ronnie Prentice opened the chute.

The poor old girl looked out at the arena again. The new weight on her back made no difference to her. But Margaret leaned forward to whisper in her ear. The cow nodded and trotted gently out of the chute. The two females made a lap in front of all of the empty stands, while Margaret turned to give us a dainty wave with her fingers, a wide smile on her face. When they got back to the chute, she hopped off her farmyard pet and trotted over to climb into the barrel, just as Old Gus had told them to do. The old cow returned to the safety of the chute on her own.

This promised to be a hell of an evening.

◊◊◊

They drew straws. As chance would have it, just like this afternoon, little Tommie Sooner won the first ride, Margaret the second. Four others had returned to ride, while three others didn't bother to show up. Any rider who stayed on through the first ride for a minimum of eight seconds would qualify for a second ride. All seconds over eight would be added to their score. Best score, plus best style, of both rider and bull, would win.

Tommie settled on the overaged bull named Diablo, precisely like he had done this afternoon. But Diablo was fidgety and nervous, not at all pleased about having a 115 pound sophomore on his back. He jostled against the sides of the chute in evil anticipation.

They opened the gate, and little Tommie went straight up into the air, like a ballistic missile being fired from a nuclear submarine. A lot of folks later speculated he spent his entire eight seconds hanging in the air. He landed with a loud splat, face down, arms and legs spread-eagled.

It looked like he was going to spend the rest of the evening on the arena floor until the pain went away. Or until the EMS came in to scrape him off the ground. But then he heard Diablo snorting around, looking for him. The clowns weren't doing a good job distracting the big guy.

Tommie jumped to his feet to dash for the barrel but ran right past it. He cleared the six foot fence at the edge of the arena by two feet. Diablo got winded chasing him. He shook his horns at little Tommie in admiration and trotted back to the holding pens.

Margaret was up. She inherited a crafty old bull named Cement Mixer. He came out of the chute spinning in tight circles, around and around like a blender working on a smoothie. Margaret kept her free arm straight up. It looked like a center pole for Cement Mixer to dance around. But he suddenly turned back, a sharp move, in the opposite direction.

It didn't fool Margaret. She hung on.

Eight seconds. Then ten. Then twelve.

She managed to swing her right leg over the left side of the bull; for a moment it looked like she was riding side saddle. She then effortlessly dropped to the ground when Cement Mixer spun to the right. Remembering Gus's instructions, she jogged across the arena to drop into the barrel. She waved at the folks in the stands before ducking down. The crowd jumped to its feet and roared. Cement Mixer looked around, totally bewildered why everyone was cheering him.

I heard a strangled *gawwk* and turned to see Gus: white-faced, holding his throat, choking on his chaw of tobacco. I pounded hard on his back, *encouraging* him to spit this time, but said, "I would say her Pa got his money's worth, Gus, even if she is just a damned girl."

Humpy

MOMMA DIDN'T WANT me to go out for football as she felt sure I would get hurt. But Pa said at five-foot-ten and 120 pounds, there wasn't enough of me to get hurt, so I might as well give it a try.

Twelve people, including Margaret Kowalski, showed up for tryouts. Margaret turned out to be our best player, except she was quick to bust you in the mouth if she thought you were putting your hands someplace you shouldn't be putting them. Coach Small told her that was gonna cost us a fifteen-yard penalty every time she did that, and we all tried to explain to her that when you were tackling someone, or being knocked down into a pile, you didn't really know where your hands were gonna go. But she didn't buy that. She said a fifteen-yard penalty was no big deal for busting a creep in the mouth and if we didn't stop it, she was gonna start swinging lower.

Anyway, I became the fill-in, meaning I was put in whenever somebody got hurt, tired, or had to leave the field to pee. I kinda liked that, as I got to practice at nearly all the positions, offense and defense, rather than concentrating on just one. Two exceptions: Coach Small never let me fill in at quarterback or center and I understood why. I couldn't see over most of the other players to throw the ball, and at center, I would be kinda like a small speed bump on a dirt road, as the opposing players ran straight over me to get to the quarterback.

Like all teams, we had *practice equipment* and *game equipment*. We never saw the game equipment until our first game. As we didn't have much of a football program, the practice equipment was a collection of leftovers from previous decades, including leather helmets in the storeroom since the 1920s, plus "later" models from the '50s, '60s and onward. In other words, if it wasn't broken, we saved it and used it. If it was broken, we fixed it. Our shoulder pads were taped together so many times that long streams of duct tape would occasionally come loose when someone was running down the field. Coach Small made it a rule that you could not bring somebody down by yanking on the tape. But that didn't apply to me as the bigger guys just pulled me along the ground, bumping along behind them while I desperately held onto the tape.

Coach brought out the game equipment the afternoon of our first game. It was beautiful. We suddenly looked like real football players. Except for me, of course. My shoulder pads extended straight out past my shoulders like flat shelves, and my hip pads drooped. We had to knot a rope around my pants to keep the weight of the pads from pulling them down. My head also swam inside my helmet like a melon in an inverted basket.

Then Coach surprised me by telling me I was going to be a *starter*. I don't know who was more shocked, me or the rest of the team. But Coach said (contritely) he was not about to go down in history as the first high school football coach in the state of Texas to *start a female*. He promised Margaret he would put her in later, and quickly, but he wasn't going to start her in our first game of the season.

Margaret's face flared crimson red as if she was going to explode. She glared at me, her eyes filled with venom. One way or another, sooner or later, I knew I was gonna pay for Coach Small's cowardice. I had beaten her out of the starting position by the sole virtue of being a male, and not much of one at that. My lips trembled, and I started to plead to Coach Small for mercy, but he shook his head, ever so slightly, to warn me not to even try. I was doomed. Margaret and I would marry twelve years later, but that is a different story.

The kick off was uneventful. It was coming right at me, but Bobby Ray Johnson stepped in front of me to snare it, thank God, then ran it down the field like a scalded dog. I was too stunned and too slow to even get into the melee. By the time I got there Bobby Ray was under a pile of players, with the referees whistling and pulling bodies off him. My macho pride told me to scold Bobby Ray for taking the ball away from me but my inner coward said to let it go, that he did a good thing, for both me and the team.

On the first play we lined up for a pass, me being the alternate wide receiver. I went with the snap. Nobody seemed to be covering me, which tells you what the opposing team thought of my talents. I looked back. But my helmet did not swivel with me. I was staring out of the small round hole on the side. I could read the words *Spalding Sports Pat. Pending* on the inside of the helmet.

And out of that small aperture, I saw the ball coming right at me.

It came in high and thumped hard across the top of my helmet. I tripped and sprawled forward face first. I hit the ground hard. The impact spun the helmet around one hundred eighty degrees. I lay on the ground for a long moment, the wind knocked out of me. But I heard people yelling, "Oh, my God, he's broken his neck!"

I did not realize they were talking about me until somebody put their hands on me, holding me down, saying in a quiet, concerned voice, "Don't move, little buddy, the stretcher is coming for you. You'll be all right."

I said, "*Mfffft.*" (It's hard to talk with helmet padding pushed into your mouth.). The hands held me down while they slid a stretcher under me. Several people lifted it up and hustled me toward the waiting ambulance. I heard people clapping and cheering for me as I was carried off the field

They nestled me into the ambulance. The siren went off and we started to move. An older man in a blue uniform said, "Don't move. We'll get this helmet off you and take a look."

It came off easily enough. I sat up quickly and said, "I'm okay, I'm okay. I was just lost in the helmet."

The two EMTs stared at me in disbelief. One of them stared at the inside of the helmet. The other touched and squeezed my neck and shoulders and asked me if I felt any pain.

"I'm okay," I repeated. "Really."

The one holding my helmet laughed and said, "You're kidding me."

Being professionals, they took my pulse, read my blood pressure, looked into my eyes with a flashlight, and felt my neck again. They gave me my helmet back, and said, "Let's go back to the game." The bastards wouldn't stop smiling.

Nobody said much to me when I walked back to our bench. A couple of people nodded. I heard a few murmurs in the crowd. One of the EMTs had a long whisper into Coach's ear, who smiled when he glanced at me and pointed to the end of the bench. We were ahead, 6-0. Margaret had scored on a long run.

The game went back and forth, with nothing much happening. Nobody got hurt, or tired, or had to pee, so I remained camped all by myself on the far end of the bench, which I knew was about as close as I was ever going to get for the rest of this game.

Then I felt something sniffing me. It was a worn out old hound dog who had wandered in past the stands when he smelled food. But he seemed fascinated by my football pants. I waved him away. He recoiled a few strides, but came pushing back, burying his nose into my leg. He then raised up—to start humping my knee.

I frantically pushed him away. But that only generated greater passion. He was humping my leg as if I was the best smelling, sexiest thing he had ever laid eyes (or nose) on. My hammering him on the head to make him stop only make him hump harder, in fear of losing me.

Then I noticed that the noise from the stands had dropped to dead silence. Also, the game had stopped, I looked around and froze (the hound dog did not). All 22 players on the field, and all 300 people in the stands, on both sides of the field, were standing stock still, staring at me and my hound dog. This display of public affection did not embarrass him.

Suddenly everyone was roaring in laugher and pointing at me. I slapped that dog, I beat that dog, I screamed at that dog, and finally stood up for better leverage to shake him off. I managed to break free and ran like hell to get off the field. My love dog followed me.

We ran past the stands, we ran out the entrance, we ran down the street, with the old mutt bellowing at me as only old hound dogs can bellow, in a mournful dirge of separation anxiety.

He finally dropped away, pulled back by the diminishing smell of the food back at the stadium. Even old hound dogs have priorities. But I kept going, all the way home. I did not return to the game. I did not return to school for a week. I never returned to practice. I had my Pa drop off the game equipment to Coach Small. No message given. None received in return.

I felt the smirks when I finally returned to the classroom. No one said anything, for a while. Then a kid in the grade above me walked over to me one day in the cafeteria and asked, "Ain't you the guy that got humped by the dog?"

I did not respond.

"Yeah, you are. Everyone's calling you 'Humpy.' Our boy 'Humpy.' But you ain't got a hump back. You got a hump leg. Oh, Lord, you gotta love it."

The name stuck. No one in school ever again called me by my real name. I was Humpy. Forever after.

I hated that name. I truly hated that name. I was pleased when Pa took a new job in Houston a year later, taking me to a new school. Far away. Where nobody knew me.

It came up again. Later. In the Army. In the chow line some guy came up to me and asked, "Say, aren't you Humpy?" I recognized him from high school. I walked away without replying, as if I had not heard him. He called after me, "Hey, I said . . ." I kept on walking.

The only one who calls me that now is Margaret, when she is really, really, angry at me. But I can live with that.

The Smile

WE NEVER MADE a great distinction between boys'
and girls' sports at our high school, as we rarely had
enough students to fill any of our teams. If we were short
on a few slots for female field hockey, we would draft
a couple of skinny freshmen boys and tell them not to
cut their hair for the rest of the season. Conversely, girls
were welcome to try out for any team they wanted, as
long as they promised not to cry if they got hurt. And, of
course, for the past four years we had Margaret.

Margaret was the standout on our football team, on
both defense and offense, the star of our basketball team,
and the mainstay on both our baseball and track teams in
the spring, when their schedules did not conflict. Which
never happened until last year, on a fine Saturday afternoon in April, when our baseball team had a home game
while, just across the road, the track team was hosting a
dual meet with the same school. We coaches consulted
over it and finally agreed that Margaret could pitch the
game and go over to compete on the track when it wasn't
her turn to bat.

That started out well. In the first inning of the ball
game she hit a home run, trotted around all three bases
to touch home, then hurried across the road to sprint
down the runway to win the long jump on her first try.

An official from Mesquite High protested that it was not right to have someone competing on the track in a baseball uniform, wearing cleats. I argued that it would be worse to have a girl on the baseball field pitching in a running jersey, shorts, and track shoes.

We reached a compromise. A small tent (that looked more like a teepee) was set up next to the track to allow Margaret to make a quick change from baseball to track clothes, then quickly revert back to baseball gear before she returned to the ball game. Unfortunately, the winds in west Texas never really die down and the damn tent blew away in a heavy gust just as she was climbing into her running shorts. Everybody on the track stopped to watch her change. As did everybody at the baseball field.

None of which bothered Margaret. She was raised with seven brothers. If any of them stared at her too long, she'd bust them in the mouth. She looked around, surprised to see everybody gawking at her, and growled. Activity on both sides of the road returned to normal.

The real trouble came in the seventh inning while Margaret was pitching. A beat-up, old, pickup truck screeched to a stop in the parking lot of the baseball field and a student from Mesquite scrambled out to hurry into their dugout. Their coach called for time out so the kid could change clothes and be substituted into the game. I didn't protest, as I assumed that Mesquite probably had trouble getting enough players to fill their teams, just as we did, and the youngster was likely coming to the game after doing chores at home.

He was a tall, good looking kid. Broad shoulders, straw blond hair, a slim waist, and a killer smile. He smiled coming out of the dugout, he smiled tapping the dirt off his cleats while he waited for his turn in the batter's circle, and he smiled at Margaret when he finally stepped up to the plate. She frowned at him and went into her windup. He smiled even wider and took one hand off his bat to blow a kiss at her.

The pitch went so wide that our catcher had to lunge far out to the right to bring it in, falling flat on his face. The Mesquite dugout hooted and laughed their heads off. The boy tapped his cleats again, smiling back at Margaret as if he and she were in this together, sharing a great prank.

Margaret went into her windup once again but was so flustered she bounced the ball on the ground, six feet in front of home plate. The umpire shouted, "Ball two."

She walked over to pick up the ball and started to return to the mound, but the ball fumbled out of her fingers. Fortunately, her back was to the umpire so she was saved from the embarrassment of him yelling, "Ball three."

I signaled for a time out. Our catcher and third baseman joined me and Margaret for a conference on the pitcher's mound. "Make him stop smiling," she said to me.

"I can't make him stop smiling," I said. "It's legal to smile in baseball."

"You gotta chew?" she asked Bobby Ray, our third baseman. He looked sheepishly at me, knowing I did not approve of our players chewing tobacco. But he pulled a plug out of his back pocket and handed it to Margaret. She took a large bite and wadded it into her left cheek. She chewed for a long moment before spitting the whole mess into the grass, offended, giving Bobby Ray the evil eye. "That shit is awful."

I said, "Watch your language."

Bobby Ray shot back at her, "You asked for it."

"Don't get smart with me, Bobby Ray, or I'll kick your ass."

"Watch your language," I repeated.

The umpire lumbered out to join us. "You people plan to finish this game or just want to stand around out here for the rest of the afternoon spitting and gabbing?"

"Make him quit smiling."

The umpire gave Margaret a blank look. "What are you talking about?"

Margaret pointed at the batter. "Make him quit smiling."

The umpire glanced over his shoulder at the boy, who smiled back at him.

"Maybe he likes to smile. Nothing wrong with that. Maybe he enjoys playing baseball. Nothing wrong with that, either."

"I can't concentrate with him smiling at me."

The umpire shrugged. "That's your problem." He turned away from us with a wave of his arm, yelling, "Play ball."

"Stay focused. That's all you have to do. Just stay focused," I said. "Can you do that?"

Margaret nodded, but with an obvious lack of conviction. We all returned to our positions.

She started her windup. The boy smiled. She stopped and stepped off the mound to collect herself. "What's your name?" he yelled out to her. Margaret fumbled the ball again. She bent over to pick it up but did a klutz kick all the way to second base.

I called another time out. The umpire groaned but allowed it.

"Do you want me to pull you? Little Tommie Sooner can take over out here."

"No," Margaret mumbled.

"Then throw a bean ball. Dust him off. Make him take a step back. That'll take the smile off his face."

Margaret blinked. "I can't do that. I might hurt him."

"It'll stop him from smiling at you."

I walked back to the dugout. She did as she was told. The sizzling pitch went straight at the boy's head. He ducked away at the last second, tripping backward and fell flat on the ground, his batting helmet spinning away.

The umpire yelled. "Ball three."

The boy got up, dusted himself off, collected his helmet, and shouted out to Margaret, "That was a good one." He smiled at her as if he really admired the way she had tried to bean him.

Margaret walked away from the pitcher's mound, coming over to the dugout. She flipped the ball to little Tommie Sooner without a word. He hurried out to take her place.

"Why?" I asked.

Margaret mumbled something toward the ground.

"What did you say?"

"He's beautiful."

"He's beautiful?"

"He has a beautiful smile."

We heard the honk of a bat hitting a baseball and I looked out to see the ball floating high over the outfield fence.

"Little Tommie Sooner couldn't handle him, either," I said.

"I'm gonna take a shower and change clothes," Margaret replied.

"What about the track?" I asked.

"I'm done for the day," she said quietly.

The game slowly drew to an end. Mesquite beat us by one run, thanks to their late arrival. I didn't think much about it. Just another game. There would be others. We would win some, lose some. No big deal. I collected the bases and carried them over to the storage locker, then straightened out the dugouts, locked the gates, and came off the field, surprised to see Margaret talking to the boy beside his battered pickup truck. She was holding herself bashfully, leaning against the truck, her arms folded, a timid smile on her face.

The Prom

BEING THE VOCATION COUNSELOR at East Jesus High School was not a great job. With few exceptions, most of the boys just wanted to be ranchers or to ride rodeo. ("I don't need algebra to talk to a cow.") Most of the girls, again with a few exceptions, only wanted to be a rancher's wife or to ride a rodeo rider. ("I don't need algebra to talk to someone who's talking to a cow.")

Being a chaperon at the senior prom was a burden that came with the job: an unavoidable, conscripted, voluntary duty. By tradition, the seniors seriously considered the senior prom to be the final exam in sex education, a subject we did not offer. But, being farm kids, most of them knew the mechanics well enough. Personal performance was tonight's real test. This exam was considered Pass or Fail, no grading, except for the discussions in the bathrooms and at the smokers' door—faculty not to be consulted.

As a chaperon, I had four duties: 1) Protect the punch bowl from alcoholic infection; 2) remind participants that slow dancing required both pairs of feet to be moving at all times; 3) prevent illegal use of hands; and 4) guard the back door of the gym against surreptitious exits.

Little Johnnie Gruber, a sophomore, caused the first ruckus of the evening. Johnnie was an exception to the rancher mind set. We assumed that one day he was gonna be either a big time entrepreneur or governor of the Great State of Texas. Tonight, without consulting any one, he set up a kiosk outside the front door of the gym, with a huge sign that said *FRESH PANTIES–Don't Let Your Momma Catch You Without One–One Size Fits All*. I was hurrying out to shut the booth down when Ms. Grindle, our art/social studies/English teacher pulled me aside to say, "He did this last year, too. Their mommas kinda like it."

"So they come out wearing a tiger thong and come back home wearing grannie panties?"

Ms. Grindle gave me a shy smile. "It's one of them 'don't ask, don't tell' things, you know what I mean?"

I poked my head out, not surprised to see that he was doing good business. Little Johnnie grinned at me like a Cheshire cat and said, "You having a good time, Mr. Dylan?" then motioned with his head at Ms. Grindle, as if she should get in line. She and I both backed away, embarrassed.

Ms. Grindle suddenly said, "Oh my God, the back door! We forgot the back door!" Sure enough, thanks to little Johnnie's distraction, the back door had been pulled open and couples were streaming out into the dark.

"Where are they going?"

"Old Mr. Detweiler's cow pasture. It's close to the gym but far enough to be away from the lights."

"They're making out in a cow pasture?"

"They're teenagers, for godsakes."

But we were too late to ward off catastrophe. Six couples were in the field when old Mr. Detweiler's bull heard noises in the night and jumped the fence to see who was screwing with his cows. Most of the kids heard him coming, chuffing and snorting, and managed to get their pants up (boys) or remembered little Johnnie's kiosk in front of the gym (girls) and took off without looking back.

Except BJ Pratt and Prudence Johnson. This was BJ's first non-solo sex experience and thought all that snorting and chuffing was coming from his classmates who were having a better time at this than he was. The big old bull started to give BJ a bovine colonoscopy, but BJ got the point and took off like a scalded cat, shedding his underwear and pants as he went. He did not return to the prom, or to the school, for a week.

Prudence managed to roll away in the other direction and cleared the four-foot fence by three feet. I made a mental note to recruit her for the track team in the spring.

Forever after, that old bull was nicknamed "Old Proc." Prudence went into the convent right after graduation, saying she "had enough sex to last me until the cows come home."

As I was returning to the gym, Mr. Townsend, the principal, came to fetch me, handing me a wooden stake. "Come along, Mr. Dylan. It's mattress time." Anticipation swept the gym. The other chaperons and remaining students trooped out of the doors to follow us to the parking lot.

Being rural Texas, most of the boys drove open bed pickup trucks, the key words being *open bed*. But none of the girls were keen to recline on the hard metal floor of a pickup truck, even if it had been cleaned of hay and horse feed. So the boys, in another East Jesus tradition, spent the prior week salvaging any mattress they could find by raiding dumpsters, roadside ditches, and the East Jesus Thrift Shop. The pickups now had wall to wall mattresses. Maybe not so clean, but softer than hard metal floors.

Mr. Townsend and I walked along, thumping the sides of the pickups with the wooden stakes, yelling, "Mattress time, mattress time." There was a lot of squealing and scrambling to straighten out clothes as the couples clambered to get away from us. Photoflashes and mobile phones registered the scene for local recorded history. The other boys, now in the spirit of things, helped us haul the mattresses out of the trucks, dragging them across the parking lot to dump them into a disorganized pile. Someone set the fire. Within minutes sparks from the great pyre lit up the Texas night sky. Kids started dancing around the bonfire, howling and singing and carrying on like the teenagers they were. Some of the girls pulled off their panties (or purchased new ones from little Johnnie) to fling them high in the air, watching them float down through the heat as they lazily settled onto the flames.

"Damn good prom," Mr. Townsend said with satisfaction. "Glad you're with us, Mr. Dylan. Damn glad."

The Farmer's Daughter

I SAW MY FIRST AIRPLANE on a late summer afternoon in 1920. I heard the metallic chunking first, like a truck engine slipping its radiator belt, then spotted the plane far out over old man Emerson's fields. The motor *chuked-chuked-chuked* while the plane weaved and waggled around up there in the sky, like it didn't belong. It grew from a speck into a fragile biplane floating in the general direction of our pasture, not making any great effort to get there.

As it was starting to land the motor went into a full roar at the wrong time, causing the airplane to streak past the pasture straight into Ma's tomato patch. And it still wasn't quite done. The engine roared again as the plane tried to power out of the tomatoes but the vines grabbed and ripped the fragile undercarriage plumb off. The plane skipped like a flat rock across our yard before ploughing straight into the pigsty.

Our hogs bolted out of the broken fence, wailing and howling like it was the end of the world. But once they hit the tomato patch, every damned one of them slammed to a dead stop. Apparently the fear of God doesn't outweigh an unripened tomato. Pa always said those hogs had less sense than a congressman in Washington.

I put down my hoe and walked over to the plane. The pilot sat stock still in the cockpit, staring at our barn wall as if he was memorizing the advertisement for *Red Man Tobacco, A Good Chew*, or admiring the painted picture of the Indian chief wearing a full war bonnet.

"You okay?" I asked.

He turned his head and used both hands to lift the goggles off his eyes. He unsnapped his leather helmet and rubbed his face and forehead as if they were really sore.

"Ma's gonna be pissed about those tomatoes," I said, trying to break the silence.

"Where am I?"

"In our pigsty."

"Do you think we could work on a broader perspective?"

"A broader perspective?" I repeated.

"Is there a name for where we are?"

"You're on the Harper farm."

The pilot gave me a thin smile. "Ah, how percipient. Is there any form of civilization near the Harper farm?"

"Oh sure. Schwarz's Junction. 'Bout a mile up the road. But it ain't much. A feed store and general merchandise emporium. But I don't think you're going to be able to fly there. It ain't got no airport."

The man unsnapped his seat belt and struggled to climb out, saying, "Let's try for a larger metropolis. One that has a restaurant and maybe a hotel."

"What's a may . . . trop . . . olis?"

"A city."

"Oh. That would be East Jesus, 'bout fifteen miles from here. They have an airport but it ain't much. An old broken down hanger and a fuel pump. But the field's flat, except for a few cows now and then."

"Oh, that's nice," the pilot said. "That may do."

"But I don't see how you gonna get there, being stuck in the pig shit like that."

"I'm supposed to be in Dallas."

I shrugged. "Guess you made a wrong turn up there somewhere."

He stepped over the side of the airplane and pulled off his helmet, and I fell in love for the first time. He was tall and lanky, with straw blond hair that matched his pencil thin mustache. His leather jacket went down to mid-thigh, covering light tan slacks that looked like a rich man's riding pants. His gloves were the same soft leather as the jacket. His boots came up over his calves. It was the first time I ever went weak in the knees for anything other than a fresh puppy dog or a newborn colt. Boys never meant much to me up to this point—they were mostly a mix of teasing bullies, moody steers, and ornery critters—but that notion came to a slamming halt for me at that moment, like them hogs in Ma's tomato patch.

"You gonna do something about them hogs?"

I nearly jumped outta my skin—someone was reading my mind. But it was just Pa. I hadn't heard him coming up behind me.

"Uh, Pa. This fella just landed in our pigsty."

"Yeah, I noticed that." He turned to the pilot. "Does mud and pig shit make a soft landing for you, son?"

The pilot smiled, and I fell even further in love. His face was sunburned and dirty from flying. The goggles had made white raccoon rings around his eyes, and his nose looked as if it had been broken and pushed back into line a couple of times. It was altogether a gorgeous smile.

"I've had worse landings, sir," he said to Pa.

"Damn, I would've liked to seen those."

"If you would help me pull my plane out and lend me some tools, I will fetch my undercarriage and wheels to see if I can repair my plane and fly away without disturbing you further."

Pa turned to survey the damaged tomato patch, the family of hogs happily picnicking in that patch, the busted fence, and the plowed trail of earth that led straight to the busted wall of our barn. "You thinking of paying for the damages, son?" he asked.

"I wasn't planning to charge you for the damages your farm did to my airplane."

Pa's face flushed redder than the tomatoes. "Say again?"

"If your farm was not in the way, I might have been able to make an excellent landing on that grassy field just over there," the pilot said, pointing to the flat pasture on the other side of the road.

I understood his logic. He had been flying low and our farm blocked his path. It wasn't like it jumped up to grab him, but it did get in front of him, maybe where it shouldn't have been. But I don't think Pa was going to buy that logic.

"Your boy saw it all," the pilot said, nodding at me. "Ask him."

It was my turn to blush from the top of my head to the end of my knobby toes. *Boy? Boy?* Just because I was barefoot, wearing bib overalls over a denim work shirt and a straw hat, and aside from the fact that my boobs were smaller than a pregnant cat's, he shoulda been able to see that I was a girl.

I took my hat off, shook out my long blond hair and glared at him.

"Oh, shit, you're a girl." he said.

That made me even madder. That's what Pa says all the time, ah-shit-you're-just-a-girl. Three boys and a girl put me on the hind tit in this family. Ma and Pa claimed they wanted another girl, and it ain't like they weren't trying, 'cause I could hear them on Saturday nights in their bedroom just above mine, but it wasn't happening yet. In the meantime I was treated like a sissy boy by everyone except Ma.

"Go get the axe, Jenny," Pa said. "We're gonna chop this airplane into kindling wood. And all that stretched fabric should burn real good, too."

"We could discuss this like gentlemen, sir," the pilot said in a quiet voice.

"You did more damage to my farm than I did to your airplane," Pa pointed out, his voice not so quiet.

"Your farm can still farm. My airplane can no longer fly."

"The axe, Jenny."

The pilot sighed. "I will pay damages, sir. Reasonable damages."

"Reasonable?"

The pilot leaned back against the side of his airplane and folded his arms. "A broken fence, some damaged tomato vines. Those skid marks have little effect on anything."

"Them hogs are eating more tomatoes than they've ever had in this lifetime," Pa said.

"Your hogs. Your tomatoes. Not my problem."

Pa managed to maintain his control. "Eighty dollars."

"Twenty dollars."

"Sixty dollars."

"Forty. But that includes dinner and a place to sleep tonight."

Pa shook his head. "You've done this before."

"One of the joys of flying, sir."

Pa fought back a smile. "We'll help you pull your plane out and fetch your wheels, and you can see what you can do about it. Then you can come in for supper." He turned to me to add, "Go fetch your brothers. They're fixing the fence out by the creek. Tell 'em we need some help. As soon as we get the plane out of this here sty, I want you to get them damn hogs back here where they belong and put the damn fence back together."

"Yeah, Pa," I replied, mortified that the pilot was still looking at me like he had never seen a girl before.

The boys traipsed in, all excited to see an airplane. They enthusiastically pulled and pushed the plane out of the sty, the pilot supervising but not doing much of the hard work.

"You got two seats in this thing?" I said in surprise, standing beside him.

The pilot nodded. "They are called cockpits. I have two cockpits."

The two older boys snickered at the word *cockpit*, and Pa slapped them both on the back of the head, saying, "Mind your manners."

"I give people rides in my airplane," the pilot explained. "That's what I do for a living. They ride in the second cockpit."

The boys nudged each other again but didn't dare say anything, trying not to smile at this new word.

Pa snorted. "Must be a thrill for them if you land like you did this morning. You charge them extra if they don't get pig shit on their shoes?"

The side of the plane said *The Great Bronson.*

"Who's Bronson?" Pa asked.

"That's me," the pilot replied.

"Damn," Pa said, laughing again.

The pilot walked away in silence to fetch his wheels.

Pa looked at me strangely, then said, "Jenny, you get them hogs back into their pen and fix that fence. And I don't want you hanging around here making moon eyes at the great Mr. Bronson. When you get done, you get back into the house to help your Ma with supper."

He walked off with the pilot, while I swatted the hogs with a long switch, herding them back to the barn. They squealed in protest and tried to outflank me but I was in a really bad mood and not about to take no nonsense from a bunch of porkers that were going to be part of my breakfast one day soon. I swatted my brothers, too, just for the hell of it. They yelled and threatened revenge but were too distracted by the airplane to follow through.

They put skids under the plane and pulled it over to the tool shed to put it up on blocks. The five of them, the three brothers, Dad, and the pilot, were now under the airplane, banging the undercarriage back into place and fitting on the wheels. All of them yelled at one another as if everyone else under there was an idiot. That's how we did things on the Harper farm.

With no one paying attention, I opened the hood (the great Bronson later informed me that on an airplane this was called a cowling) to peek at the engine. It was a little fancier than your tractor, but it looked like it would work the same, so I fiddled with some of the moving parts, then pulled off some of the hoses to look at them.

"What are you doing?" the Great Bronson asked in an annoyed voice, inching out from under the plane.

"Your radiator's cracked and your propeller is split in two and your fuel line is clogged and your fan belts are frayed and loose. Other than that, your engine looks okay."

"What the hell do you know about airplanes?"

"Nothing. But I know tractor engines."

"She damn well does," Pa said. "If it's mechanical, Jenny can make it work. Makes the boys madder than hell."

"We can fix most of that," I said. "But I think Pa should charge you extra."

There was a long pause before the pilot said, "How long will all of that take?"

"Day or two."

"I'm supposed to be in Dallas before that."

"Guess you're gonna have to walk," I said.

"She is definitely your daughter," the pilot said to Pa.

Pa laughed again. "I knew that." But I was puzzled by the comment. If I weren't Pa's daughter, who would I be?

Anyway, the pilot stayed for two days while we fussed and hammered and glued and bent parts back into place, and in the evenings after supper he told us stories about flying over France in the Great War. The boys hung onto every word, and I could see Pa becoming impressed with the Great Bronson, the war hero who claimed to be an ace that shot down a dozen Germans.

But he behaved himself. Polite to Ma at the dinner table and drinking only a little 'shine with Pa on the porch before going out to the hayloft after everyone got tired of talking.

I became restless, moody, and irritated, and Pa said I wasn't fit to be around. But he said it kindly as if he knew what was wrong with me.

On the last night on the porch, the pilot told us that his plane was called Jenny, too.

"You named your plane after a girl named Jenny?" I asked, crestfallen. He was in love with another girl.

"No, silly," he said. "The plane is a Curtiss JN4, a plane we used quite a bit in the war. But everybody nick-named it 'Jenny' for short."

"How about that, Jenny?" Pa said. "A plane named for you."

I looked at the airplane standing next to the tool shed and memorized its long frame, snub nose and trim wings and thought it was the most beautiful thing I had ever seen.

In the morning, everyone agreed we were done. The Great Bronson walked around the plane jiggling the wings, thumbing the wires, wiggling the tail section, then came around to the front to admire our handiwork. "On to Dallas," he finally said.

"Watch out for them farms and ranches over that way," Pa said. "Don't let them get in your way. They got some pretty big tomato patches over there."

"Anyone want a ride before I leave?" the pilot asked. But he was getting to know Pa, as he added, "For free?"

Pa backed away. "No thanks, son. I saw you land one time and that didn't inspire a lot of confidence."

But the boys were all over themselves, shoving and pushing like boys do, ready to resort to fisticuffs to establish priority.

"Jenny?" the pilot asked.

I looked at Pa. He smiled at me. "You're a big girl. Do what you want."

The two older boys went first, and then little Buck and me. It was cramped, but we wedged ourselves in and managed to buckle the seat belt. I forgot all about that as the plane raced along the ground to lift into the air. I discovered that love was not a lanky blond pilot with a handsome pencil thin mustache. Love was scattered puffy clouds in an endless blue sky, with the earth isolated and small below us.

The pilot did barrel rolls, *Immelmann* turns and loops, then swooped low while me and little Buck waved crazily at Pa and Ma.

The Great Bronson shook Pa's and the boys' hands and kissed Ma and me on the cheek. My knees went weak, but I managed to keep my feet.

Away he went, the plane lifting off the grass and climbing high until it turned into a speck going east toward Dallas.

I left the farm a few years later. Ma and Pa decided that I should go to that teaching school back East. It was something that women could do to get off the farm. My two older brothers eventually moved on to their own farms and ranches. Little Buck hung on with Ma and Pa. I eventually got a teaching job–in Dallas. I never came across the Great Bronson again.

But I did manage to save enough money to take flying lessons. In a Jenny. They were calling it an "old Jenny" by then, but that didn't bother me. It still had its long frame and snub nose and trim wings, and it was beautiful. And my love continued to blossom among the scattered clouds in an endless blue sky, with the earth isolated and small below.

Acknowledgements

These stories were previously published, awarded, or presented as follows. All copyrights are retained by the author.

"Bridge," Stage Performance, Liars' League, Hong Kong, June, 2014

"Carjacking," *Bethlehem Writers Roundtable*, http://bwgwritersroundtable.com, Bethlehem Writers Group, LLC, Issue No. 9, June, 2012

"Car Wash," *Over My Dead Body: The Mystery Magazine Online*, http://www.overmydeadbody.com/, June, 2012

"Convenience Store," *Hardboiled Crime Scene*, Dead Guns Press (2015)

"Dead Man Breathing," *Trails End*, Zimbell House Publishing, LLC (2018)

"The Farmer's Daughter," *Once Around the Sun: Sweet, Funny, and Strange Tales for All Seasons*, Bethlehem Writers Group, LLC (2013)

"Getting There," *One-Star Reviews of the Afterlife*, Alternate Hilarities Vol. 5, Strange Musings Press (2016)

"Initiation Night," Honorable Mention, Writer's Digest Popular Fiction Awards, May 2010; *Over My Dead Body: The Mystery Magazine Online*, http://www.overmydeadbody.com/, May, 2013; 2nd Place, "Best Crime

Story on the Web," The Bullet Awards, (formerly at http://thebulletawards.blogspot.com) May, 2013

"On the Skrang," *River Tales*, Zimbell House Publishing, LLC (2017)

"Only a Game," *Once Around the Sun: Sweet, Funny, and Strange Tales for All Seasons*, Bethlehem Writers Group, LLC (2013)

"The Prom," *Bethlehem Writers Roundtable*, http://bwgwritersroundtable.com, Bethlehem Writers Group, LLC, Issue No. 11, August, 2012

"Sisters," *Bethlehem Writers Roundtable*, http://bwg-writersroundtable.com, Bethlehem Writers Group, LLC, Issue No. 47, Winter, 2017

"The Smile ," *The Write Connections*, Greater Lehigh Valley Writers Group (2017)

"Suicide," Stage Performance, Liar's League, London, April 2009; *Bethlehem Writers Roundtable*, http://bwg-writersroundtable.com, Bethlehem Writers Group, LLC Issue No. 6, March, 2012.

"They," *The Deep Dark Woods*, Revolving Door Press (2015)

"The TruckStop Heist," (originally entitled "The Wawa Heist"), Honorable Mention, Writer's Digest Popular Fiction Awards, 2017

"The Viewing," *Over My Dead Body: The Mystery Magazine Online*, http://www.overmydeadbody.com/, September, 2011

I would like to thank the wonderful people at the Bethlehem Writers Group LLC, for their guidance and care in pulling this book together. I particularly want to thank Carol L. Wright, Marianne H. Donley, Dianna Sinovic, and Emily P. W. Murphy for the time and thought and effort they have put into this book to make it a reality. I also want to thank the Bethlehem Writers Group for the coaching, critiquing, and inspiration that they have provided over the years.

About the Author

In an effort to support his addiction to writing, Jerome W. McFadden has sold carbon black in Africa, boogie boards in Europe, and crayons in Asia. These efforts have led him to long term residences in Istanbul, Casablanca, Paris, and Singapore, as well as short stays in Houston and San Francisco. He now resides in eastern Pennsylvania.

These writing efforts have brought a swath of awards and honorable mentions from a wide range of writing contests, including a Bullet Award for the best crime fiction on the web in 2009; appearances in a wide range of e-zines, lit magazines, and anthologies; plus the reading of his stories on stage by the Liars' League Hong Kong and London. All of which has taught him not to leave his day job.

He is currently a member of the Bethlehem Writers Group (http://bethlehemwritersgroup.com) and the Greater Lehigh Valley Writers Group (http://glvwg.org), and is a frequent contributor to the *Bethlehem Writers Roundtable* (http://bwgwritersroundtable.com).